TIMMY AND THE TIGER

by Marjorie B. Paradis

Pictures by Marc Simont

THE JUNIOR LITERARY GUILD
AND
HARPER & BROTHERS, NEW YORK

To Steven

TIMMY AND THE TIGER

CHAPTER 1.

IT TOOK an age, Timothy had discovered, to move to the country. First he thought his father and mother would never find a house they liked; and even after they had bought one in Bedford, which was forty miles from New York, nothing much seemed to happen. They'd drive up on a Saturday and maybe there would be a little fresh paint somewhere, or men working in the cellar, but nothing very exciting.

Then suddenly, three days ago, things had begun to disappear: the books from the bookshelves, the dishes from the pantry, their clothes from the closets. And yesterday his sister Helen had vanished—gone for a visit, and a good thing, too; for when you were moving, a little girl of three could be an awful nuisance. Tomorrow the van would come for the furniture and the Harper family would be leaving the city forever.

Timothy had made up his mind long ago that once they'd moved to the country he was going to be different; he'd live up to his age and his parents' expectation of him.

"Now you're ten years old, you're quite a man," his father had said on his birthday early in December, as he tightened the strap of a new wrist watch. "And a man such as your mother and I want you to be is honest and truthful—which is part of being honest—and brave."

Of course he was honest (he wouldn't steal anything), and he tried to be truthful; but secretly he knew he was not brave, and the thought filled him with shame. He had so many fears. Not that he ever told anyone about them; but often he cried out in his sleep, awakening his parents as well as himself, which was such a baby trick.

He sometimes thought the trouble lay in the fact he was small for his age, the littlest boy in his class and awfully skinny. Recently, when he had complained about his size to his mother, she had said, "Someone has to be the smallest, and you'll suddenly sprout like a beanstalk. I can tell because you have such big feet. In fact, I was telling your father, you're beginning to grow very fast."

If he was beginning to get tall, he ought to begin to get brave and moving to the country would do it. He would leave behind everything that frightened him.

He sat at his desk that last afternoon filled with happiness. Although nothing in school had changed, it seemed quite different, exciting, like the apartment which was in no way like their old home.

Timothy pulled himself out of his daydream at the sound of his name.

"Timothy Harper is leaving us today. Let's wish him a lot of happiness in the country." The teacher started clapping and the class joined in with vigor while Timothy sat pleased and embarrassed. He hadn't known they cared that much about him. As the class filed out, the teacher met him at the door and shook hands with him.

"I'm going to miss you very much, Timothy," she said.

He mumbled his thanks and went out in such a daze he even forgot to dread the sudden appearance of Butch, who seldom allowed him to reach home without one good punch.

"Guess you won't like starting a new school very much," suggested Charles, walking with him as far as the corner.

"I'm not going until September. Mom'll teach me the rest of this term."

"Lucky bum. Wish I was moving to the country," said Charles.

"Yeah, it's nice." Timothy thought about adding, "Maybe next fall I'll go in for athletics." But he was afraid Charles would laugh. Also, at that moment, he remembered Butch, who was hiding somewhere waiting to spring out at him when he was alone.

"Say, Charles, come on home with me and see our place. It looks as funny as anything, all torn up."

"Can't. Mom said to come right home. So long, Tim. Have a good time."

"So long, Charles, old boy." Timothy walked on straight and proud. He wasn't afraid of Butch. Tomorrow he would be leaving him forever.

Within a block of the apartment, just as Tim was hoping for the best, Butch jumped out from somewhere and started to walk beside him. Older by a year, large and thick-set, he could have bullied almost any boy in the class, but all winter he had devoted himself to Timothy.

The first time Butch had knocked him down, Timmy had run home, blood from his nose mingling with his tears.

4

"I'll teach you to protect yourself," his father had promised, and had bought a pair of boxing gloves. The lessons were worse than Butch. Timothy's wrists were so thin the gloves wouldn't stay on. He hadn't the slightest idea what his father meant when he talked about warding off a blow or giving an uppercut, so he would shut his eyes and strike out blindly. After the first boxing lesson, although Butch continued to pester him, Tim said nothing about it, and soon the lessons ceased.

Now, without so much as a glance at Butch, he increased his speed until his green corduroy slacks rubbed noisily. Butch took longer steps.

"So mama's pet is moving to the country to milk the cows!" Butch laughed. "That's a joke, you milking a cow—you wouldn't dare milk a butterfly."

On Timothy hurried, knowing it would come any minute. There! Tripped from the back, down he fell.

"I'm going to miss you," Butch said, as Timothy slowly got to his feet. A punch sent him down for the second time.

"And for good measure, so you'll remember me . . ." Butch yanked off the red ski cap, tossed it under an oncoming automobile, dusted his

5

woolen gloves, and sauntered off in the opposite
direction.

Timothy rubbed most of the tire tracks off his
hat, put it back on, picked up his lunch box, and
hurried toward home, relieved it had been no
worse. Ahead of him awaited another worry. The
self-service elevator. He hated it! Often he waited
in the foyer and chatted with the doorman until
someone else was going up. But today he had an
idea for an electric derrick, and he thought how
pleasant it would be to work without Helen

6

around. So, impatient to get busy, he gathered his courage and made the ascent alone. The trip up was never as fearsome as going down.

He found, to his great disappointment, that all his things had been packed. Davie, who went to kindergarten, sat cutting pictures from a magazine. That might interest *him*, but not Timothy. He tried playing Lone Ranger among the barrels and boxes, but it needed three for a decent game. Much to his surprise, he found he actually missed Helen! Yes, it seemed strange without her. He hadn't supposed her absence could make the family seem so shrunken.

That night Timothy, who was always the first up, got permission to set his alarm clock for five-thirty. He stayed awake a long time, going over with satisfaction the things he would be leaving behind, things he feared.

There was the old paper man. He wasn't so afraid of him any more, but he used to be years ago when his father walked with him to school.

"Run ahead and get me a *Times*," his father would say, giving him the money. The paper man, sitting in his little wooden house, looked to Timothy like a lion in a cage, with his shaggy gray hair, shaggy mustache, and shaggy beard all mixed together. But what made Timothy feel queer in his

7

stomach were the old man's eyes. Their centers, instead of being back, were white, like the buttons on Timmy's undershirt. Timothy didn't speak of it for a long time, but when he did, his father said, "Yes, the poor man's blind."

Blind! If you thought about it, it was awful. Timothy knew because he tried walking with his eyes shut. Now and then, out of sympathy, he left a nickel of his own on the tin plate. Once he got to the country, he could forget all about the blind old man.

Another thing, he'd never have to go in the subway. At first he had loved the subway. He liked to stand by the front door and watch the red lights turn green.

Then one day he had asked his father, "What would happen, Dad, if the train went so fast the red didn't turn green?"

"That," his father had said impressively, "would be just too bad."

And Timothy knew what he meant. A terrific, frightful smash-up. After that he hated the subway. When he *had* to ride it, he did what he could to help the lights turn. Under his breath he would beg, "Turn green, turn green." Sometimes he would say he was too tired to stand, but he felt even more uncomfortable sitting down, as if he weren't doing his part, as if it would be his fault if the rocketing car smashed to smithereens. Well, there would be no subways in the country.

No Butch and no self-service elevator and no . . . no . . .

When the alarm finally went off, it was black as pitch.

"Get up, old sleepyhead," he said to Dave, who lay in the next bed, snuggled down so that only a wisp of fair hair showed. "Don't you hear me? Get up. We're moving to the country today." And he ripped off the covers, exposing the huddled figure of Dave in striped pajamas.

Timothy ate breakfast standing. No one objected, and he enjoyed the change. He also liked the paper plates, which made the food taste quite different.

"Let's go downstairs and watch for the van," Davie suggested.

"No, we'll look from the window," insisted Timothy, thinking of the elevator.

Used to being bossed, David readily agreed, and the boys clattered over the bare floor to the living room. The view from the eighth floor, cut off as it was by the wings of the apartment house, proved too limited.

"This is no good. We ought to go down on the

street," Timothy announced, as if the idea were his own.

Glad to have them out of the way, Mrs. Harper tossed them their windbreakers.

Out in the hall Timothy assured himself he had got over being scared of the old elevator and boldly pushed the button. But when the yellow light filled the ground-glass door, try as he would, he could not prevent the knot from forming in his stomach.

"Come on, you," he said roughly to David, and swung open the door.

"Let me do the button. I know which one," begged Davie.

"No, you can't." Timothy shut the folding gate, put his finger on the first floor button, closed his eyes and pressed. A soft rumble of weights, a creak of machinery, and the elevator slowly sank, while Timothy's heart mounted until it fairly choked him. This time it might happen! It probably would, just for spite, because he was leaving it forever. The nasty old thing . . . any moment . . . any second it might drop.

The noise gave way to stillness. They had reached the foyer. They were safe! He flung back the gate with a brave sweep of his arm and opened the door.

"Last one to the street's a stinker!" Relief lent wings to his feet, and he dashed down the foyer, but the doorman stopped him.

"Hey, you kids, think you own the place?"

"No, we own a place in the country," David answered proudly.

"And that's where you belong, all you youngsters, and all dogs, too." The doorman glared down at the two boys, one fair, the other dark, and his face softened. "Not that they don't come worse than youse, but keepin' kids in an apartment's like keepin' bees in a thimble."

"I guess my mother wouldn't like that very much," agreed David.

A woman the boys called Mrs. Franz Joseph came out of her apartment on the first floor with a big police dog straining at his leash.

"Now calm down, Franz Joseph," she said.

"Stay back, Davie," ordered Timmy, as he went up and stroked the dog's head, proud of his courage.

"I like boys who like dogs." Mrs. Franz Joseph flashed him a smile.

"I like dogs too," grumbled Dave.

"He's little, and he might get knocked down," Timothy said protectively, as they all went down the steps.

Mrs. Franz Joseph went off with the dog, and Timmy and David sat down on the steps to wait for the van. In a little while Gracie Garwood came out with the doorman, who was carrying her doll carriage. He set it on the sidewalk with a thump and glared at the boys as if they were at fault.

"See what I mean 'bout kids?"

"Cranky old thing," said Grace, when he had returned to the foyer.

"We're moving to the country today," said Dave.

"I know. Glad I'm not." She tossed her curls.

"Why?" Timmy asked.

"Because there are snakes in the country, that's why."

"Are you afraid of snakes?" Timothy's voice was full of scorn.

"'Course I am." She set her doll straight and tucked in the knitted afghan. "So are you."

"I am not." Timothy got to his feet as if he were going to make a speech. "I'm not afraid of *any-thing* in the country."

CHAPTER 2.

LOOK, Timmy! Look, it's coming! The van! I saw it first!" Davie shouted.

Sure enough, a truck big as a garage was coming slowly up the street. The boys waved to the three men who sat in front, and they waved back; but the driver continued on past the house.

"Oh, heck," wailed Dave, on the verge of tears. "Come back. Come back," he shouted.

Obediently, the van stopped, backed up, and swung around at right angles to the curb.

"He never would have stopped if it hadn't been for me," boasted Dave.

Timothy knew better, but sometimes he didn't bother to argue.

Ordered by the largest of the men to stay out of

13

the way, the boys perched on the brick wall near the entrance.

Their familiar furniture, set out on the side-walk, looked strange and pitiful.

"Is that mommy's desk?" asked Dave.

"Of course."

"What's that funny-looking thing?"

"The dining room table, taken apart."

But even Timothy found it hard to realize that the shallow box covered with green felt was ac-tually their piano without any legs. Why, when they had played Indian and camped under it, it had seemed enormous!

Their father joined them, and he, too, laughed at the array of furniture. "Looks as if we'd been dispossessed. I'm going for the car. Want to come?"

The invitation, usually a treat, was refused. But a few minutes later, when their father returned with the car, they unwillingly abandoned their post and went upstairs with him.

The apartment, empty of everything but a few boxes and stacks of pictures, looked entirely differ-ent. There seemed to be many more doors, more hall, more space. A lonely airplane calendar hung on the boys' bedroom wall. Timothy, filled with pity for it, took it down and tucked it under his windbreaker.

14

After a final check had been made to be sure that nothing had been overlooked, the boys ran to the front window to see what was happening in the street. As they watched, the last of the Harper belongings disappeared into the van and the men fastened the iron bolts on the doors. The motor roared, the top of the van quivered as it strained away from the curb, and finally the truck rumbled off down the street.

"Nothing to do now but go," Mr. Harper said.

"We've had a nice life here, Joe. Seems kind of sad." Mrs. Harper sighed as she said it.

Timothy knew exactly how she felt and pressed the crackling calendar close to him.

The ride to Bedford, although it was only forty miles, seemed to take forever. Impatient to get to the new house, Timothy objected when they stopped in a drug store for lunch. He couldn't even enjoy the chocolate ice cream soda.

"While we're here, we'd better have some sandwiches made for our supper," suggested Mr. Harper.

"But, Joe, if we take too long, the van will get there first," objected Mrs. Harper before Timothy could protest.

"Never fear, it won't. The men'll want their

lunch, too; and they can't go on the parkways, so it'll take them longer."

So they waited for sandwiches to be made, and Timothy wished he hadn't gobbled his soda.

Finally they were off again. Davie napped by the window, but Timothy, fearful they might have taken a wrong road, kept a sharp lookout for a familiar landmark.

At last he saw the railroad station—*their* station now—and then *their* drug store.

"Next stop the Harper residence," called his father, like a conductor.

And sure enough, a few minutes later they passed the big white stucco house where the well-known wild game hunter Martha Gates lived— when she wasn't in the wilds of India—and turned up their own drive!

Their new home, which was really quite old, gleamed with fresh white paint and glossy green shutters. It was a simple square house, such as the boys usually drew, with two windows on either side of the center door and five windows on the second floor. The attic had windows only on the sides.

Mr. Harper stopped the car at the flagstone walk that led to the front entrance. Timothy poked David with his elbow, and the boys were out of the car with the last turn of the wheel.

"This m'lads is your ancestral home," their father said jokingly, "about which you can brag to your children's children."

"Not me," grumbled Timothy. "I'm never going to get married."

"You'll miss a lot," his mother said, as she stood in the cold February wind gazing at the house. "Oh, Joe, it really is a sweet place."

She seemed as near tears looking at the new house as she had been leaving the old. Timothy could not understand it at all.

"Hurry, Dad, unlock the door."

His father took out a bunch of keys, shook them, and selected one. At the door he paused. "Remember, boys, no scraps, no squabbling. A home's as good as we make it."

He unlocked the heavy door, and the boys dashed in. Timothy paused at the sound of his mother's laugh and looked around to see his father carrying her into the house, as if she were Helen.

"Why, Dad?"

"For good luck," answered his father.

The house had a center hall and four rooms on each floor, every one of which, except the kitchen, had an open fireplace. Originally, their father said, that had been the only way to heat the house.

Mrs. Harper liked the way the cleaning woman

had left the place; Mr. Harper liked the way the oil burner worked; and the boys liked the stairs—Timmy for a secret reason of his own and Dave because he had used them so seldom. Up and down they clattered, from attic to cellar, darting from room to room.

"Why don't you take off your windbreakers and hang them in your closet?" their mother suggested.

When Timothy pulled off his jacket, the calendar fell out, and he got his mother's permission to pin it on his wall. It gave him a pleasant sense of possession.

"Here comes the van," shouted his father, with all Davie's enthusiasm.

Unloading proved even more exciting than loading. Timothy and Davie found themselves quite useful. "Show the men your rooms, boys." "Show them Helen's room." "Show them our room."

In an astonishingly short time the empty house became a furnished home. The men laid the rugs, turned the green box into a piano, and the slats into beds.

Soon after the men left, it began to get dark; and Mr. Harper went around the living room connecting the lamps and lighting them.

"I never dreamed we'd accomplish so much the first day," said Mrs. Harper, straightening her
18

tired shoulders. "How about eating our supper in front of the living room fireplace?"

"Hold your horses, my dear." Mr. Harper was now stuffing the newspapers they had used to wrap the dishes into an empty barrel. "This is an occasion—our first meal in our new home. I'm going to the village for ice cream. Anyone want to come?"

There was an immediate "I do, I do" from the children and eventually Mrs. Harper said she'd go too.

They had often been to the village during their trips to the house, but now it was different. This was *their* village. Only the drug and stationery stores were open, so while their parents bought the dessert, the boys studied the plastic cars in the stationery window, choosing the ones they would buy when they got their allowance.

As soon as they got back from the village, Timmy helped his father lay the fire, while Davie and Mrs. Harper went to the kitchen to get some plates. Then, grouped cozily around the roaring fire, with the windows reflecting the light like black mirrors, they ate their sandwiches and ice cream—their first supper in their new home. Timmy enjoyed watching the leaping flames and didn't gulp down his dinner as he had his lunch.

"Well," Mrs. Harper said soon after they'd fin-

ished eating, "it's bed for you young laborers."

"Let's go out and smell the good earth first," suggested Mr. Harper.

So they all put on coats and went out in the back yard.

"Sniff," he ordered.

They obeyed.

"Isn't it wonderful! Look at the sky."

Overhead thousands and thousands of stars glittered brightly against the black velvet sky.

Timothy took one look, then lowered his eyes. He had forgotten how he felt about stars. When you were in the city, there didn't seem to be so many and they didn't glow so vividly. Now he remembered how last summer at camp he had suffered the same sense of terror. There were too, too many. Each star, his father had said, was as big or bigger than the earth. Many of them spun around and around up there in the sky. Suppose one fell and crashed into them! It would only take one, and there were so many!

"I miss Helen," said his mother, and he wondered if the stars made her feel something like the way he did.

"I suppose so," his father replied cheerfully. "But it's been a great help missing the little miss. Come, boys, and hit the hay."

Slowly Timothy followed them in. All joy had vanished. The shame he had suffered in the city once more possessed him. He realized he had taken one of his fears with him to the country.

CHAPTER 3.

Helen would be coming home with her father on the commuters' train. They had moved only five days ago, yet it seemed to Timothy like a lifetime. He had to stretch his memory to recall the apartment, school, even Butch. He felt he had always lived here in the country, and he loved it. He loved the freedom of being able to dash out the kitchen or front door, without any doorman to stop him. He loved having plenty of room in the old barn for his bike and his tools and batteries. And as the house became more settled, he found he even loved the return of order. There was the problem of the stars, of course, but he tried to forget about that.

And now, in an hour or so, Helen would be back. Like his mother, he had missed her, which

seemed queer; for before she had always seemed to be in the way.

They had spent the afternoon, he and Dave and his mother, settling Helen's room. Her little dresses had been hung neatly in her closet; her dolls had been set out on top of the low bookcase and her books arranged on the shelves. Mrs. Harper had made up the small bed with crisp sheets and the blue spread she had embroidered that depicted Mary and her little lamb.

With some time to spare, Timothy suggested that he and Dave make pictures for Helen's pink walls. Dave, who specialized in trains, quickly reproduced a snorting engine that filled the bright blue sky with inky smoke. Timothy labored long on a red schoolhouse with a green roof, toward which Mary and her lamb were walking. His mother said it was one of the best pictures he had ever drawn, and he felt a great satisfaction as he thumbtacked it over Helen's bed.

At last, in the blackness of night, they waited at the station for Helen's arrival. The boys had treated themselves to chewing gum from a slot machine, and Timothy had postponed the purchase of a plastic roadster to buy a whole box of Chiclets as a coming-home present for his sister.

"Will she stay when she comes, Mommy?" asked Dave.

"Of course she'll stay, Davie." Mrs. Harper's eyes were damp. "I didn't know I could be so busy and at the same time miss her so much."

Timothy chewed his gum understandingly.

"Would you miss me?" asked Dave, who wanted everything clear and definite.

"I certainly would," replied his mother, pressing his towhead to her side. "When you boys were at the hospital having your tonsils out, I felt so strange; as if something were wrong, as if I'd gone out without my dress."

Timothy laughed so loud she had to hush him.

In a few minutes a gong clanged and they could hear the approaching train rumbling in the distance. Then, preceded by a glaring searchlight, the monster thundered into the station and grated to a stop in a swirl of dust and paper. Timmy tried to ignore the feeling in his stomach. He wasn't afraid—not *really* afraid. Besides, he was too old to grab his mother's hand, as Davie had done.

The instant the train stopped, men carrying newspapers dropped off the steps; then came the women with handbags, who descended more carefully. But where was Helen?

Timothy darted down the platform from car to

24

car. Suppose she were not on the train, or suppose the snorting old engine puffed off with her still inside! He ran back to his mother.

"Have they missed it?" she asked, as if he knew the answer.

Timmy couldn't believe it. But maybe Helen would never come. Maybe she'd been run over on the way to Grand Central! If only she would come, he'd never be cross with her again!

Suddenly his face brightened, and he shouted, "There's dad!" But where was Helen? Then his father set the blue suitcase he was carrying on the platform—and, yes, there was Helen, jumping into his father's arms. It was all right. Everything was perfect!

Timothy hung back and greeted her last.

"Hi, Hel." There was no enthusiasm in his greeting; he merely chewed vigorously.

She flung her arms about him; her little white-gloved hands pressed into his waist. "Timmy, I love you. Got any goom for me?"

He drew out the box.

"You children and your gum," his father said laughingly. "Come along."

The house became brand-new to the boys again as they showed it to Helen. Greatly excited, they tried to show her everything at the same instant.

"Look at the fireplace, Helen. We toast marsh-mallows."

"Look at the kitchen stools. We eat breakfast at the counter."

"Look at the stagecoaches on the dining room wallpaper." "Look at . . . Look at . . ."

"How about letting Helen see her own room?" suggested Mrs. Harper. "Come on upstairs, dear."

The boys dashed up ahead, and Timmy watched his sister's blue eyes as she gazed about the pretty pink and blue room. His picture looked even better than he had remembered.

"It's nice. I love it." Helen smiled and showed her dimples.

"I made that train for you." Dave pointed out his work of art.

"It's awful nice. I love it."

Timmy waited for her to admire his offering, but she didn't even notice it, so he went into his room and sulked. Helen trotted contentedly downstairs with her mother for an early supper.

After a while, his mother called him. "Tim, aren't you coming down? Helen's telling us about her visit."

"I'm busy," he shouted back.

Mrs. Harper sighed and said to her husband,

"That funny boy of ours. I'm sure he missed Helen as much as any of us."

Having Helen back with them was just about all the Harpers needed to feel really settled, and Timmy soon got over being hurt because she hadn't noticed his picture right away.

One evening a week or so later, Timmy begged his mother to let him get his father's breakfast the next morning. "It's a cinch, Mom. Nothing to it. Guess I can put out fruit juice and corn flakes and boil an egg and make instant coffee.

"Imagine me lying in bed while you do my work, Timmy."

"But I'd like to. Honest I would."

"Well, if you really want to, Timmy. I'll be glad of the chance to sleep a little later."

The next day when his father came down to breakfast, Timothy had everything ready on the yellow linoleum counter. It was lots of fun eating breakfast alone with his father. He could talk to him about electricity, a subject which fascinated Timmy. After that morning, they always had breakfast together.

As a result of their early morning conversations, Timmy's father helped him rig up a primitive communication system between the house and the

27

barn. Consisting of two bells, some wire, and some old batteries, it enabled Timmy to ring a bell in the barn from the kitchen and a bell in the kitchen when he was in the barn. He usually used the bells to summon Davie from one place to the other. If for some reason Davie appeared without being summoned, he was sent back to wait for the official buzz.

But a really big job awaited Timothy and his father, the men folk, as his father called them. It was about time for them to start work on the vegetable garden. The March earth was still too hard to start preparing the soil, so they got busy building a wire enclosure.

One Saturday afternoon when Timothy had been left to put away the tools, a boy appeared at the split-rail fence that separated the Harper property from the wood beyond.

"Hello, there," the boy called. "Who are you?"

He was older than Timothy, a thick-set boy with disagreeable lips. Something about him reminded Timothy of Butch.

"I'm me," answered Timothy ungraciously.

"Come over here," ordered the larger boy.

"I will not." Timothy stooped and picked up a saw.

"Will you come if I give you this?" The boy

produced a chocolate candy bar from his pocket and balanced it on the fence.

"Sure," Timmy said, dropping the saw.

The candy was not snatched away, as he had anticipated, and he picked it up. The boy brushed away his offer to share it.

"Eat it all. I have millions of 'em. What made you so nasty?"

"You reminded me of a kid I knew in the city."

"You didn't like him?"

"No, I didn't."

"Why not?"

"Because he used to— Just because."

Timmy knew it would be a mistake to admit the truth, but the boy guessed it.

"Used to beat you up, I bet. You're so skinny it wouldn't be hard."

The bigger boy looked at him through narrowed eyes. "What's your name?"

"Timothy Harper. What's yours?"

"Don't you know me?" The boy straightened. "I'm Alec—Alexander Atkins." When Timothy bit into the candy without saying anything, Alec added, "We're the Three A's, my father, mother, and I. Alice, Alf, and Alec."

"So what?" asked Timothy and took another bite.

"Are you pretending you never heard of us?"

"Never did."

"Never heard of 'Breakfast with the Three A's'?"

"Nope."

"Gee, you're stupid." But then Alec said in a friendly voice, "Come on over and I'll show you where I live."

Timothy hesitated, crammed the rest of the chocolate bar into his mouth, and climbed over the fence.

"This way," ordered his neighbor, preceding him through the thicket.

"Nice woods," praised Timothy.

"They're ours—fifteen acres; and next to us is the Reservation—thousands of acres." He sounded as if he owned the Reservation, too.

They made their way through the thicket to a narrow path, which they followed until they came to a clearing in the woods. Ahead of them Timmy saw a rambling log house surrounded by a white picket fence.

"See that big, mammoth house?" Alec's voice had lost its pleasant tone. "That's mine. It cost my father thousands and thousands. That's where we broadcast every morning to a million people, and you say you never heard of us."

"Never did," repeated Timothy.

"Well, you've heard of us now, and you won't forget us, see?" He gave Timothy a punch that sent him over backward. "It's no wonder you get knocked down, whether you're in the city or the country, with such a name!"

"My name's all right," muttered Timothy, getting to his feet and backing away.

"Sure, it's just right for you—you said it. Timothy . . . I bet you're called Timid."

Timmy wasn't positive what "timid" meant, but he was sure he'd been insulted.

"Don't you dare call me Timid," he retorted.

Though he spoke boldly, Timothy continued to shy away from the older boy.

"Run home to your mama, Timid," jeered Alec, as he let himself through the fence.

Timid . . . timid . . . timid. Timothy repeated the word to himself as he retraced his steps through the woods. Each time he said it, it sounded more horrible.

That night at dinner, he asked his parents, "Ever hear of the Three A's?"

" 'Breakfast with the Three A's' Certainly," answered his mother. "They live around here somewhere."

"And who, pray, are the Three A's?" asked Mr. Harper.

"They're on the radio, Joe. Alice, Alf, and Alec. You know them, dear."

"Never heard of them," he denied.

Timothy giggled. Would Alec, he wondered, if he'd heard his father, try to punch him, too?

Before he went to bed that night, he found a small dictionary and alone in his room looked up the name Alec had called him.

His mouth tightened as he read the meaning: Fearful, faint-hearted. See cowardly.

Cowardly—how had Alec known?

CHAPTER 4.

"LISTEN to this, Joe." Mrs. Harper, who had been studying the Sunday advertisements, paused to read a news item. " 'Mrs. Martha Gates, who has been in India for the last three months buying elephants for a circus, returns home this Saturday. It is said she will bring a Bengal tiger as a house guest.' " Anxiety edged her voice. "You don't suppose she'll keep it here, next door?"

"Probably," her husband answered calmly.

"Well, I can't say I like that very much."

The boys, playing with their electric trains, which their father set up every Sunday, sat back on their heels to listen.

"A tiger isn't as dangerous as a panther," said Timothy, turning off the transmission.

"I think you're wrong there." His father got up,

scattering newspapers on the floor, and took a large book from the shelf. "Let's look it up."

He pushed his spectacles higher on his nose and turned the pages. "Here you are. 'The tiger is considered the second most dangerous feline animal' —feline includes the whole cat family. 'The lion comes first, then the tiger, and then the panther.' It says here that the tiger can be more dangerous to humans than the lion, because it will kill even when not hungry. It speaks of a man-eating Bengal—"

"Joe!" called his wife. "Are you trying to scare us to death?"

"I'm only quoting facts, Peggy. Don't you want your children to be intelligent? As for our neighbor, if there's any truth at all in the news, you'll find it's only a baby, a cub."

"I love babies," murmured Helen, washing a tiny doll in a wee tub.

Timothy, who had felt a return of the old stomach pinching, drew a breath of relief and started up the engine. A little cub wouldn't be bad.

"What do you think of these curtains, Joe?" Mrs. Harper again interrupted her husband to get his opinion. She was going to the city the next day for her first shopping excursion and to Timothy's

great disgust had engaged a sitter. Mrs. Lauderbach, who had been highly recommended by the
agency, had the added advantage of owning her
own car and would not have to be picked up.

When Timothy had said he would look after the
children for nothing, his mother had flatly refused
his offer. "Thank you, dear, but I wouldn't be
comfortable."

Now, still annoyed by her lack of confidence in
him, Timothy chanted, "Oh, Mrs. Lauderbach sat
on a tack."

"And her head she did crack," added his father.

"Joe, please," begged Mrs. Harper. Then, ad-
dressing the boys, "Remember, you must be polite
to her. We haven't much choice here in the country, and we'll have to like what we can get."

The next morning all three children—even
Timothy—waited on the edge of the road for the
arrival of Mrs. Lauderbach.

"Wonder if Mrs. Lauderbach will sit on the floor
like Kate," mused Davie, thinking of the high
school girl they used to have.

"She ought to. Sitters ought to sit," affirmed
Timothy.

"Maybe she'll take us for a ride in her car," suggested Davie.

"Maybe, maybe," sang Helen, holding Timothy's hand and hopping on one foot. "I like her. I like her a lot."

"You don't know her yet," scolded Timothy.

"Yes, I do. I like her. I like everybody who has a car."

A glittering red automobile approached them and slowed down.

"Wowie! A Mercury! Some class!" announced Timothy, who knew the makes and relative values of all the recent models.

But the driver only waved to the children and drove on.

When Mrs. Lauderbach finally arrived, a rattle and roar, a clanking and sputtering announced her approach. The ancient Chevy, rusty and dilapidated, with one fender missing and the others liable to drop off at any moment, turned up the drive. Running after it, the three children arrived at the back of the house at the same time as the car.

They stood in a row and watched her emerge. First the door swung open crookedly, then a vast black rear protruded; an enormous leg, ending in a sturdy oxford, felt for the ground, followed by its mate. Then the rest of Mrs. Lauderbach appeared. The gray hair on her round head was sparse as sand grass. Her black coat glittered with brass but-

36

tons and was topped by a flaming red scarf. She
had a large mouth and a nose so small it seemed

scarcely adequate to support the nickel spectacles.
From within the car, she drew out a cord-handled
paper bag as fat as herself.

"Hello, children. I'm Aunty Lauderbach."

"Hello," answered Davie.

"I like you; I like you very much." Helen's dimples showed as she made her usual speech.

Timothy gave the woman a searching look and
turned toward the house. "I'll tell my mother
you've come."

When he had made his announcement, he
headed for the barn, where he summoned Davie by
means of the electric bell. Helen arrived with Dave.

"She's too fat," said Timothy.

"Yes, she's awful, awful fat," agreed Helen.

Davie looked hopefully at his older brother.
"What can we do about her being fat?"

"We can act bad so she'll never come again."

"But mommy said we had to be nice."

"Not me," affirmed Timothy. He turned away
and started to work on an auto he was making out
of a crate.

In a few minutes his mother came into the barn
to get the car.

"I'll be back around four o'clock, and I'm expecting you to be good." When she said the last,

she looked straight at Timothy. He lowered his eyes.

"She's the worst of all," he said, viciously hammering a nail.

"Nonsense. She seems very nice."

"Nice and fat," snorted Timothy.

"Yes, she's awful fat," repeated Helen.

"She can't help being fat, dear."

" 'Course she can," contradicted Timothy. "She eats too much. She eats like an elephant."

"Now, Timmy, you mustn't talk like that," his mother said firmly. "I'm sure if you're nice to her, she'll be nice to you." She kissed them all, Helen last. "Take a long nap, precious, and I'll be home by the time you wake. Bye, boys. Be good. I made chocolate pudding for dessert."

When they had waved a final farewell to the disappearing car, Timothy announced they would go in and play chair-train. This game, long ago banned by their mother, used to be a great favorite of his. They scampered indoors and started shoving all the chairs on the first floor into a line, even the kitchen stools. Soon the line stretched all the way across the width of the house: living room, hall, and dining room.

One chair only they could not use. Mrs. Lauderbach occupied it and refused to transfer herself and her sewing to the couch.

"I like it better here by the window," she said stubbornly, and went on with the sewing she had brought in the paper bag.

If there'd been a real train in the house, it couldn't have made much more noise than Timmy's chair-train. Its bell clanged often and violently, and the chug, chug of the wheels was deafening. Timothy, finding it a strain on his throat, got a tin lid and beat it with a spoon. The combined confusion would have disturbed most people, but not Mrs. Lauderbach.

She sat and sewed; broke her thread and unwound more. She stitched and hummed without apparently hearing a sound.

"I'm tired of this, let's go out," suggested Timothy. When Davie started to replace a chair, he was told, "Leave the train alone. We might want to play later."

David, who knew they were supposed to clear up the things from one game before they started to play anything else, hesitated. Then he got into his coat and followed his brother.

At noon Mrs. Lauderbach called them in for lunch. Four doilies had been set on the dining room table and on each was a plate well filled with meat cakes, boiled potatoes, carrots, and peanut butter sandwiches.

"Looks as if we'll have to sit on our thumbs," Mrs. Lauderbach said cheerfully.

"I'm eating on the train." Timothy, hearing no objection, picked up his plate and fork and carried them to one of the chairs. The other two did the same. Helen's potato fell off, but she put it back on the plate.

"A new experience for me, eating on a train." And Mrs. Lauderbach, to Timothy's surprise, joined them. "Where does it go? I have to be back by four o'clock."

"It goes to Chicago," said Timothy. "And we won't be back for a week."

"Chicago! Land o' love! I never was so far. Don't you have tables on your diner?"

The suggestion appealed to Timothy, and he brought over some small tables and arranged them so that everyone had a place to put his plate. Out of pride in his train, he even went so far as to distribute napkins.

"Now isn't this pleasant," said the sitter. "I always wanted to eat in a diner. See the telegraph poles fly by?"

The idea of pleasing her spoiled everything for Timothy. He decided on more violent tactics.

41

"My meat cake's too rare." He stood up, plunged his fork into Davie's, and lifted it onto his own plate.

David's astonishment gave way to fury. He let out a piercing shriek. When this produced no result, he wailed, "Timmy took my meat cake! He took my meat cake!" Mrs. Lauderbach continued to eat contentedly, and Davie yelled a forbidden word. "You stinker! You stinker!"

No one came to his aid, so Davie jumped up and made a dive for Timmy's plate. In the scuffle two tables were overturned, one of the dishes was smashed, and food was scattered across the living room rug.

"There! *Now* see what you've done," Timmy said to Mrs. Lauderbach. "I guess my mother won't like *that* very much."

"We never do like it when we make a bad job," replied the sitter. Then, seeing that Helen was engaged in a minor skirmish with her boiled potato, she leaned toward the little girl and said, "Let Aunty Lauderbach mash it for you, dear. Except for you, precious, Mrs. Harper's made a wonderful bad job of bringing up her children."

"She has not," defended Timothy. "When she's home, we don't act like this. We're good. You're

42

not much of a sitter. You're supposed to make us behave."

"Not me," said the sitter calmly. "I brought up my own four children good, but I learned long ago that a few hours isn't long enough to turn wild hyenas into saints." She lumbered out of her chair. "Come on, Helen, let's visit the milk bar."

While Mrs. Lauderbach and Helen stood at the dining room table drinking milk, the two boys stared at the mess they had made.

"Let's be savages and eat from the floor," suggested Timmy.

"What did she say about mommy?"

"Nothing that was true. It was a big lie. She lets us be bad, then she blames our mother."

The boys managed to eat most of their food, pausing now and then to pull rug fluff out of it.

Timothy picked up the broken china and took it to the garbage pail; he returned with the carpet sweeper.

"We can be as good as anyone else, if we want to," he grumbled.

"Sure we can," said Davie.

"Let's put back the chairs. I'm sick of this game."

The house soon resumed most of its usual neatness. The furniture, except for the two chairs that

Helen and the sitter had reoccupied, had been put back more or less in place; and Timmy had run the carpet sweeper over the living room rug.

"See?" Timothy hissed at Mrs. Lauderbach.

She looked over her spectacles and nodded. "Not bad. Give Aunty your plate, Helen baby, the boys want to put back our chairs. Shall we eat dessert in the dining room?"

"How does it look now?" demanded Timothy when she came in with the four puddings.

"Like calm after a hurricane. When my kids did something good, I used to reward them with a story. After I get what's left of the dishes washed, maybe you'd like me to tell you a story."

"A make-up?" asked Timothy.

"That's right."

"About an auto—a big bus?"

"Sure, if you like. I make 'em to order."

"That's what I want."

"Then that's what you'll have. If you kids was to help with the dishes, I'd get through quicker."

They all pitched in; Helen dried the silver and Timothy the dishes, and Davie put them away. In no time at all Mrs. Lauderbach was seated in her chair, Helen on her lap, the boys on the floor before her.

44

She told them a very exciting story about an enormous bus that got out of control in hilly country and rolled over three counties. It ran over corn fields and potato patches, on and on, down one hill and up another. Davie giggled with glee when it smashed a hut belonging to a wicked miser and sat motionless with fear as it approached a lovely little white church with a beautiful spire. Timothy listened with interest—a kid story, but not so bad. Mrs. Lauderbach explained how much the church meant to the townspeople, how even the children had given their pennies for its construction; and now it lay directly in the path of the oncoming bus! The villagers could see it coming and frantically tried to think of something to do. Then, when the bus was about halfway down the long hill leading to the village, a little boy shouted, "Come on, everyone! Quick! Bring your mattresses and throw them in a pile." So they all rushed to their homes and dragged out their mattresses and heaped them up in front of the church. And just in time! The bus whizzed down the street and crashed right into the mattresses. Some of them burst open, scattering cotton and horsehair all over the street and on some of the villagers. But the bus had been stopped and the church was saved.

"You tell nice stories," said Davie.

"Been doin' it for many years. I've better ones than that."

"Tell us another," ordered Timothy.

"Nope. One at a time. That's my rule."

Instinctively he knew she meant what she said, so he didn't bother to tease.

"Now lovie-lamb has to have her nap. If you want, Helen, I'll sing you a funny song when you get in bed."

"Can I listen?" asked Davie.

"Sure, why not? Both of you."

She sang about a monkey who married the baboon's sister, and the children laughed noisily.

"You boys," she said when they were downstairs again, "ought to know Charlotte Gates. There's a wonderful girl! I go there every Thursday, when her governess is off. Shows how grand she is—her mother's been away for months and she's good as gold."

"She lives next door," Timothy said. "Her mother's going to bring home a wild tiger, and they're even more dangerous than lions."

"Maybe she is and maybe she isn't. Want me to telephone and see if she'll be there? Your mother said you could go if you liked."

"I have too much to do," said Timothy.

"What toys she has!" Mrs. Lauderbach rolled her eyes.

"I don't like girls' toys."

"She has boys' toys, too. A big two-story garage filled with cars. It has an elevator you can pull up and down."

"Let's go, Timmy," coaxed Davie.

"How old is she?" demanded Timothy.

"Eleven."

"We might go for a little while," he conceded.

Charlotte answered the telephone. The boys could hear her, and it was evident by her voice that she actually liked Mrs. Lauderbach, whom she called Aunty Lauder. She said she'd love to have the boys come over. She wanted to get acquainted.

"Before my children went visiting, I saw that they washed their hands and faces," said Mrs. Lauderbach when she'd hung up.

"So does our mother," bragged Timothy.

"You know, Timmy," she said, "I might have been mistaken. Maybe I'll find she hasn't done such a bad job with you children after all."

CHAPTER 5.

THE big white house, pure as a monstrous wedding cake, was an impressive sight. Approaching it up the curved blue-gravel drive, the boys were awed by its grandeur. The house was fronted by a sweeping semicircular porch, with columns two stories high, and was surrounded by a huge bright green lawn. Some sheep were nibbling on the lush-looking grass.

"Like a castle," muttered Davie, feeling for Timothy's hand.

"Castles have moats to keep out the enemy. This is more like the White House in Washington." Timothy, too, felt slightly overwhelmed and paused uncertainly. A flagstone path leading to the rear cut across the lawn. Probably they should use the kitchen door.

48

While Timmy was wondering what to do, he heard the sound of someone knocking on glass. Looking up, he saw a round, merry-faced girl at one of the windows. She waved to them and pointed to the front door.

As the boys were mounting the shallow steps, the wide mahogany door was flung open and the girl called, "Hello, there! Come on in."

Her plumpness reminded Timothy of Mrs. Lauderbach, and the full skirt of her checked blue and white dress did not make her look any slimmer. Short dark pigtails hung back of each ear. Her face was wide, her smile broad, showing white generous teeth. She wasn't pretty, nor little and dainty, but she looked so pleasant, so different from the flouncey, silky girl Timothy had expected, that he liked her immediately.

"Hello," he said, all shyness gone. "Guess you're Charlotte."

"Right. And I guess you're Tim."

"Timothy," he corrected, hoping she would never know what that nasty boy had called him.

"I like your name." She smiled down at Davie and patted his hair. "I like your name, too, David."

"How do you like Mrs. Lauderbach?" Davie asked abruptly.

49

"Aunty Lauder? I love her. Did you ever hear her laugh?"

"No," admitted Timothy, thinking she had had little to laugh about in his house.

"And she tells the *best* stories," added Charlotte.

"Yes," he agreed. "Her stories are all right."

She led them along the broad hall and up the wide carpeted stairs. The rooms they had passed on either side of the hall looked to Timothy like those you might see in a palace.

"Big, isn't it?" Davie rolled his blue eyes.

Charlotte nodded. "Dad says we're two peanuts lost in Yankee Stadium. But it will be different after Saturday. My mother's coming home."

"My mother's away too," said Davie.

The brown eyes softened sympathetically. "I know, but not for long."

"Until four o'clock. That's long."

Charlotte laughed and paused at the top of the stairs to call for Miss Sayer.

"I had to figure out for my arithmetic this morning how many hours it would be until mother returns, and then how many minutes. But the minutes made it seem longer than just five days."

"Pooh, a minute's nothing," comforted Timothy.

"But an awful lot of minutes is something," she argued.

He nodded. "Only it never seems as long when you don't have to say, 'A week from—' "

"That's right," she agreed. "It's this Saturday, day after, day after, day after, day after tomorrow."

He liked this girl, liked her very much, and he didn't believe a word about that tiger business. Mrs. Lauderbach had said she had a good mother, and no good mother would bring a wild animal to live with her daughter.

A pretty young woman in a pink dress came to meet them.

"This is Miss Sayer, my governess," introduced Charlotte. "The big boy is Timothy and the little one's David."

"I'm big for my age," protested Davie.

"Indeed you are," agreed Miss Sayer, who had no way of knowing how old he was. She smiled pleasantly at Timmy and then said to them, "If you play nicely together, we'll all have a tea party at three o'clock."

She left the children and they climbed the next flight. These stairs were bare, and the boys felt more at home.

The playroom, Timothy decided, was even

larger than the assembly room at his old school. It was filled, as he had been promised, with toys of all kinds. A complete toy shop! Helen would have made straight for the dollhouse, which was taller than he. Davie sat adoringly before the garage Mrs. Lauderbach had so faithfully described, but Timothy's eye was caught and held by a wooden train with cars large enough for even him to sit in. Its tracks ran around the room in a great oval.

"Not a bad train," he commented.

"I've just repainted the cars. My father made them for Jack."

"Who's Jack?"

"My brother."

"Didn't know you had a brother." Maybe he'd be horrid like Alec.

"Jack died." She spoke softly and lowered her eyes.

"Oh." A deep sadness overwhelmed Timothy. It was bad enough to die—awful—too awful; but to die and leave such wonderful trains! Like the stars in the heavens, it was something he didn't want to think about.

"When?" he asked.

"Four years ago."

"Oh, a long time ago." That made it better, much better. Why, it was ages ago; before Helen was born. "Are you allowed to play with his trains?"

"Of course."

"Then let's. I'll be the engineer; you two can be passengers. Come on. We'll go to San Francisco."

They each sat in a car, Timothy taking possession of the locomotive, which had a loud bell and a whistle. The train had pedals like a chain velocipede; and when they all worked, they made pretty good time.

"Now it's David's turn to be engineer," Charlotte said when they had been around the room twice.

Timothy, who preferred giving orders himself, hesitated before getting out of the favored seat. Then he agreed. "O.K. That's fair."

They played train and they played with the garage and Charlotte even made them play house.

Three o'clock came amazingly soon and with it Miss Sayer carrying refreshments. These were served on Charlotte's red and white dishes at a small dining table set in one corner of the playroom. Miss Sayer sat with them, but Charlotte poured the cocoa and ladled out the whipped cream.

"You ought to see Aunty Lauder on one of these chairs," she giggled.

"They must be awful, frightful, terrible strong," said Dave.

"That's what she says. My father made them, and he's proud as anything they hold up."

"Is your father a carpenter?" asked Davie.

"Kind of. He has a regular shop in the cellar."

"Silly," protested Timothy. "Dad said he's president of the Carbide Company."

"Oh, sure. That, too," Charlotte said. "But I like best what he makes."

"Well, he must make a lot of money and I guess you like that too."

"I get an allowance," boasted Dave, interrupting the discussion. "I get five cents a day when I'm good, and Timmy, he gets ten. Maybe we won't get any today." And he sighed.

"Were you naughty?" asked Miss Sayer.

"Kind of—to Mrs. Lauderbach. But Timmy was worse'n me."

"And of course she'll snitch," grumbled Timothy, wishing he could make his brother stop calling him Timmy.

"No, she won't," corrected Charlotte. "Her way's worse. She'll expect you to tell."

"Huh," sniffed Timothy. Silly old thing; she could go on expecting. "And suppose I don't?"

54

"Then I guess she might not come again. She says all children who are brought up right are good. And when they're good, it's easy for her; and she only wants easy places."

"I don't blame her," said Miss Sayer with a laugh.

When they had finished the cookies and cocoa, the governess went off with the pitcher, the plate, and the cream bowl, leaving them to wash the dishes.

"In a big house like this I should think you'd have servants to do the work," grumbled Timothy.

"Work! Washing these dishes? It's fun." Charlotte opened a double door behind the table, revealing a small sink.

She was right; it did seem like fun. She washed and the boys dried; and when they were through, she insisted on washing the dishtowels and the napkins.

"I want everything neat as pie when my mother comes," she explained, as she hung her wash on the towel rack. "Know what she's bringing?"

Timothy shook his head. Charlotte couldn't mean the wild tiger.

"A lion?" queried Davie.

"No, a tiger."

Then it was true!

"But it's only a baby tiger," said Timothy. "And a cub couldn't hurt you."

"It isn't such a baby any more I don't think."

"But he'll be kept in a cage, won't he?"

"He'll go in the animal room, like all the others. She always brings home something queer. Last time it was a kangaroo. I'd like a kangaroo better than a tiger." Timothy suspected she too was afraid. Why shouldn't she be? A wild tiger in her own house! Did she know a tiger was more dangerous than a lion?

"Want to see his room?" asked Charlotte. "It's downstairs, next to mine." That made it worse, much worse.

They followed her to a barred doorway on the floor below and looked about the strange room. The walls had been painted to look like a forest and dark green linoleum covered the floor. A hollowed log used for an eating trough stood beneath one of the grated windows.

Timothy felt his stomach turn over; his heart thumped in his throat. And he had thought he had left all that behind him in the city. But who ever expected to live next door to a wild tiger?

"Oh, dear, you can't squeeze me in? How about next week?"

Timothy saw Mrs. Lauderbach shake her head, and he lowered his eyes and kicked the leg of the counter with his saddle shoe.

"It's not that I'm too busy," explained the sitter. "But I don't seem to be the one for the job." She smiled contentedly.

Timothy tightened his lips.

"Oh, dear, dear," lamented his mother. "Don't you think you can cope with them?"

"Seems maybe as if I couldn't," agreed Mrs. Lauderbach with her usual cheer.

"Of course three are a handful," admitted Mrs. Harper. "Can I say anything to make you change your mind—just for one more time?"

"She won't come because we were bad," Timmy burst out. "We played train all over the house and I took Dave's meat cake and we had a fight and spilled our dinner and broke a dish."

"Oh, boys! Boys!" cried their mother. "No wonder you hesitate, Mrs. Lauderbach."

"Oh, I could forget all that." Mrs. Lauderbach brushed it away with a sweeping gesture. "It's just that I was brought up not to go where I'm not wanted. Now if the boys was to want me—"

59

"*I* do," insisted Timothy.

"Me too," chimed in Davie.

Mrs. Harper looked at them uncertainly. "You've been so highly recommended, Mrs. Lauderbach."

"Me? I'm only good with good children."

"We'll be good," promised Timothy.

"We'll be awful, terrible good," promised Davie.

Mrs. Harper smiled at her sons. "They usually are really very good. Suppose you try it again Thursday, the same time."

"She can't come Thursdays," Timothy answered for her.

Mrs. Lauderbach smiled broadly. "He learns fast, that boy. I could make it next Friday."

"All right, Friday then."

"And will you tell us a story about a lion?" asked Davie.

"A lion it'll be." She lumbered to the door, the floor shaking under her.

When the rattle of the ancient car had died away, Mrs. Harper returned to the subject of their bad manners.

"I'm terribly disappointed," she sighed.

"Do we get any allowance?" Dave preferred knowing the worst.

"Most certainly not. You were both very bad.

Whether or not she's a good sitter, it doesn't excuse you."

"She's not so bad," said Timothy.

"Maybe not," his mother said uncertainly. "But I dare say we can find one you'll like better."

"We like her," defended Timothy. Davie echoed the statement.

"Well, you're the funniest boys," said their mother. "You never liked anyone in the city until I found Kate, who was young and thin; and now you insist you like this—er—plump—"

"She can't help being fat," interrupted Timmy. "She's all right."

"We'll see how things go Friday. Now I must go up to see Helen. I hear her calling."

At dinner that night the boys were questioned about their visit.

"We had whipped cream and she has every toy in the world," David said.

"Poor child. With her mother away at the ends of the earth, she ought to have something," sympathized Mrs. Harper.

"Her mother'll be home Saturday." It seemed awfully close to Timothy as he said it.

"Trailing her tiger behind her?" his father asked.

"Joe, you don't suppose she actually *will?*"

Without waiting for a reply, she turned to Timmy and asked, "You didn't hear anything about it, did you?"

Timothy nodded and bit into his bread.

"You did? Is it true?"

Again he nodded.

"Answer, Timmy. Don't always nod." But before he could speak, she turned to her husband and said, as if he were responsible, "Something must be done, Joe. This is a residential district in a civilized community. I'm not going to be worried to death about a savage animal every time Helen goes out to play."

"And do you imagine your sons could cope with a Bengal tiger?" he teased.

Creeping fears gathered within Timothy's thin frame.

"No joking, Joe, can't we get up a petition or something and make her get rid of it?"

"When you're mad, Peggy, your eyes shine like diamonds." He smiled across the table. "Don't worry about the tiger. It's only a publicity stunt. In a couple of days or a couple of weeks it'll go to the zoo, poor beggar."

Comforted, Mrs. Harper resumed eating her dinner. But not Timothy. He had no wish for food. Hadn't he seen the room? People didn't go to all that work for a few days.

Although the subject was not discussed again for some time, the fear had taken root. Often in the night Timothy would see the escaped tiger leap over the dividing hedge and seize Helen by the throat.

That Friday a false spring shot up the thermometer, so Mrs. Harper had agreed to a picnic lunch on the south side of the barn. She had suggested inviting Charlotte by telephone, and the girl had accepted readily. Now, as the boys were spreading auto robes on the grass in preparation, a distant rattle of tin announced that Mrs. Lauderbach was approaching.

When she clambered out of her car, all three children, as well as Mrs. Harper, were waiting to greet her. Helen, grabbing her legs and hugging them, nearly toppled her on her nose.

"Easy to see the children like you," said Mrs. Harper.

"Sure they like me." Mrs. Lauderbach hauled her bag of sewing from the car. "Either I get along with them or I get along." Her laugh rippled from her neck to her stomach.

Charlotte arrived with the noon blast of the fire

horn, bringing with her a three-layer chocolate cake.

"Will you tell us a story while we eat?" asked Timothy when Mrs. Lauderbach came out with the lunch.

"Me sit on the ground! I'd never get up. Not till doomsday. You'd have to feed me out here and bring me an umbrella when it rained and cover me with a blanket when it snowed." She winked at Charlotte. "But maybe your mother'd know how to haul me up. She's used to elephants."

"I'll get you a chair," offered Timothy.

"Well, now, that's something else again. Sure, I'll be delighted to join the picnic."

Timmy scampered off and returned with a rocker.

"It's going to be about a lion," Davie told Charlotte.

"Oh, I like fairy princes," objected the girl.

"Bless your heart, this is about both," Mrs. Lauderbach reassured her.

So, while the children ate their sandwiches, hard-boiled eggs, and bananas and washed them down with milk, Mrs. Lauderbach, pausing now and then for a bite herself, told them about a lion that escaped from the circus. Her imitation of the lion's roar rivaled the fire horn and delighted the children. Although a hundred men and boys tried to capture the beast, it got away from them and ran into the woods. At last they all gave up, except one small boy. Panting and puffing, on he kept; but the lion got further and further away. Getting deeper and deeper into the woods, the little boy eventually came upon a fairy prince in white armor. (Here Mrs. Lauderbach paused to smile at Charlotte and to take a drink of milk.)

" 'You're a plucky little boy,' said the prince, 'and I'm going to give you something to help catch the lion.' " She viewed her audience. "Guess what."

"A sword, a flaming sword," suggested Charlotte.

"A gun?" queried Davie.

"Nope. Wings. Little wings for his feet that fitted on like rubbers."

"How could he catch a lion with wings?" scoffed Timothy.

"He couldn't," agreed the storyteller. "But with them he flew through the woods like a bird until he hovered over the lion. Then, as you say, he wondered how he could catch it. Now just beyond the wood was the seaside, and suddenly he spied some fishermen drying nets. Quick as a mosquito's wink, he flew over to them and borrowed one. Back to the woods he soared and dropped the net over the lion. He had him caught, safe and sound. Then the fairy prince appeared again and took back the wings. 'You're a very fine boy,' he praised. 'You didn't give up like the others. You'll get along in the world; for you will find, if you keep at a thing, you're bound to get help.' " Mrs. Lauderbach clapped her hands to show that that was the end.

"He was brave," commented Davie.

"Sure he was brave," she agreed, cutting the cake.

"Wish I was," said Charlotte.

"Now like I told you yesterday, don't you worry your head about that tiger. Your mother'd never bring it home if it was dangerous."

"She likes dangerous animals. Once she brought a monkey."

Timothy snickered. "Monkeys are fun."

"Not this one. It scratched me and pulled my hair and tried to bite me."

"I like monkeys very much," Helen cried. "I love monkeys."

"You're nothing but a lot of monkeys yourself," called a voice from the woods, and over the log fence climbed Alec Atkins. "You're making an awful lot of noise. What d'you think you're doing?"

"We're having a picnic, Alec, and you're not invited," Charlotte said severely. Then she softened. "But you can have a piece of cake if you want."

"Cake? I can get all I want home." However, he cut himself a thick wedge. "A lousy place for a picnic—in the back yard."

"Behave yourself, Alec, or go right home," said Mrs. Lauderbach.

"I'll go home when I feel like it," he snapped.

Timmy, forgetting how rude he himself had been to Mrs. Lauderbach only a few days ago, was shocked by this impudence.

"It's like I always say," sighed Mrs. Lauderbach. "I can't get along with children who have bad parents."

"Who says my parents are bad?" Alec glared at her.

"You do, by the way you act," the sitter answered firmly. She took Helen on her lap and started to rock and hum.

Alec stared at her in a towering rage, his face gray-white like the paper plates.

"You can't get away with a thing like that, you—you—sitter!" As the chair rocked backward, he gave it a yank; a harder yank, perhaps, than he intended, for the rocker toppled over, sliding Helen and Mrs. Lauderbach to the ground. The sight of the big woman sprawled on the grass, a swirl of

67

black wool and pink rayon, her two enormous legs kicking wildly, sent David into a burst of laughter. Helen joined in, jumping up and skipping about.

68

Anger, on the other hand, possessed Timothy. He wished he were big and strong enough to do something to Alec. Charlotte, having the same reaction, gave Alec a shove with all her considerable weight, toppling him over and herself on top of him.

"Help me," she called, while her prisoner kicked and yelled.

Timmy straddled Alec's heaving chest and managed to pin the thrashing arms under his sharp knees.

"Good, good for you," cheered Mrs. Lauderbach, getting to a sitting position.

"She can't say I have bad parents," bellowed Alec.

"She can too," snapped Timothy. "They must be bad to have you so nasty. And they're not so important either. My father never even heard of them. So there."

He felt grand sitting on top of the bully.

"Let me up, you're squashing me," sobbed Alec.

"Say you're sorry," ordered Timothy. When the ugly mouth remained set, he grabbed the two ears and thumped Alec's head on the ground. "Say it. Say it."

"I'm sorry," mumbled Alec.

"All right. Let's let him up, Char."

Alec scrambled to his feet and retreated a safe distance.

"Sissy, sissy," he called back. "Had to have a girl help you. No wonder you're named Timid. No wonder! But you'll be sorry—just wait. You'll be sorry, Timid."

CHAPTER 7.

THAT night Timothy dreamed Alec owned a tiger and that he brought it to the log fence and sicked it on him. He could see the bared teeth, hear the lashing of the tail accompanied by a throaty growl. He tried to run away but found it impossible to move a muscle. There he stood, as the animal slunk toward him across the grass. When it made a spring for him, he let out a shriek that awakened everyone in the house but Davie.

His father came in, preceded by the beam of his flashlight.

"What's the matter, son? Bad dream?" Mr. Harper sat on the edge of the bed and slipped an arm around the hunched shoulders.

"Guess so." Timothy wanted to cling to his father but instead hugged his own thumping chest.

71

"Lie down now, Timmy, and I'll cover you."
The boy obeyed. "How about it? Everything all right?"

"Sure. Sure, Dad. Sorry I woke you."

"That's nothing." His father gave the top of his head a farewell pat and went back to his room. Timmy hated to see the light disappear. Sissy! Imagine a big boy of ten wanting a night light.

He wished, oh, how he wished, he were brave! But even if he were, could he help his dreams? Or were brave people also brave in their sleep? Charlotte's mother, for instance. He was lucky his mother didn't go off to buy elephants; lucky, too, he didn't have parents like Alec. Maybe brave people always felt as he had when he sat on top of Alec! That had been wonderful! But Alec had called him a sissy—also that other awful name—and Charlotte had heard him.

There were tears on Timmy's pillow when he finally fell asleep.

The next morning, while he was dressing, he saw Charlotte and her father drive off to the airport. Let them bring back the tiger; he wasn't afraid. Indeed, in the light of day his dream seemed very silly.

Right after breakfast, the boys and their father went out to work on the vegetable garden, and they spaded away busily all morning. They had just had lunch and gone back to work again when they heard a car come up their drive.

"I warned everyone in the city to stay away until April," grumbled Mr. Harper, turning over a clod and powdering it with his spade.

A few minutes later Mrs. Harper called from the kitchen door, "Joe-o-o, boys, come in, company!"

"Guess those are orders," groaned Mr. Harper, driving his spade into the earth. "Follow along, boys."

"Maybe we'll have a tea party," said Davie.

But even that prospect didn't cheer his father.

"Whoever it is, it's no friend of mine, Peggy," he muttered, as he came in the door.

"Hush, Joe. It's the Congregational minister, Mr. Judson. Boys, roll down your dungarees and wash your hands. That goes for you too, Joe."

Timmy trailed into the living room last and was introduced to a thin old man in a Roman collar and clerical clothes. His sparse white hair stood up like starched threads, his eyes glistened as if they had been polished, and his smile was friendly and warm. Timmy could tell he smiled a lot from the deep wrinkles on the sides of his mouth.

"How do you do, Timothy," he said, shaking Timmy's hand. "Slender lads like you make me feel comfortable. I was the skinniest boy! Legs like broomsticks. And in those days we wore short pants until we were fourteen or fifteen—would you believe it? Once, I remember, when I was going to a party, I wound a pair of long ribbed stockings around my spindleshanks, fastened them with a safety pin, and covered them with another pair. Alas for my pride! The underneath stockings slipped down around my ankles, and I looked like a spavined donkey."

They all laughed appreciatively, but Timmy roared so loud and so long, his mother finally had to hush him. He didn't know what kind of a donkey Mr. Judson had been talking about, but he knew that he must have looked very funny with the stockings all bunched around his ankles. He had never imagined a minister could make you laugh so hard.

"I heard of you people through my advance scout, Mrs. Lauderbach," explained Mr. Judson. "You'll find it hard to live up to her praises. She considers you a wonderful family."

Timmy, sitting on a stool, smiled his satisfaction.

"Mrs. Lauderbach seems like an unusual woman," his mother said, and to this Timothy nodded his agreement.

Mr. Judson nodded also. "Very. Very unusual.

Put her four children through college on the point of a needle."

"Oh, was she a dressmaker?" his mother asked.

"Yes. She still makes underthings for children."

So that was what she was sewing on all the time, Timmy thought.

"Very picky and choosy about whom she'll sit for, too," went on the minister. "I've suggested she might be a good influence on bad children, but she claims the parents are to blame and she can't influence *them* because they go out as soon as she arrives."

They discussed Mrs. Lauderbach for a few minutes more, and then Mr. Judson announced the main reason for his call. He had come, he said, to invite the boys to lunch on Monday so they could meet his two grandchildren.

"We have a girl a little larger than you, Timothy. She's ten. How old are you?"

"Ten."

"Um, I see. Well, girls get big first. The boy is smaller than David. He's five."

"I'm five and big for my age," said Davie.

"So you are. Anyway, I'm sure you'll all enjoy one another. My grandchildren are a little homesick, and you boys can probably cheer them up."

He paused for a second, then added, "Oh, and I had a special request from Mrs. Judson to ask the little girl too—for *her* to play with she said."

"Not all three!" protested Mrs. Harper.

"I hear them coming," interrupted Timmy, and he rushed to the window in time to see the Gateses' car turn up the circular drive.

"Has she got the tiger?" asked Davie, nearly tearing down the new chintz hangings in his scramble to get to the window. "Yep, that must be it in that big box in the trailer."

Mrs. Harper's lips tightened, and she looked a little wan. Not trusting herself to make any comment about the goings on next door in front of company, she turned to Mr. Judson and spoke of something else.

The boys watched the car until it disappeared up the drive and then drifted back to the others. Timmy was having trouble with his stomach again and was quiet for the remainder of the minister's visit.

"Well," said Mr. Judson a few minutes later, "it's time for me to be getting home. Sharpen your appetites for Monday, boys." He stood up and reached for his coat. "When I married the village belle, I didn't know I was getting the best cook in seven counties. Take my advice, boys, and look into that before you take a wife. You might not be as lucky as I."

"Don't bother to warn Timmy," Mrs. Harper said with a laugh. "He's never going to marry."

"Give him time," said Mr. Judson, hunching into his coat. "He'll realize someday that a happy home is the nearest thing to heaven on earth."

They all walked outdoors to see him off. Getting into the car, he paused a minute and said, "Oh, by the way, Mrs. Lauderbach says your youngsters will be joining our Sunday School in the autumn. Why not start them now?"

"We'll have to put our own money in the collection," Davie said, offering one good reason for the delay.

"Shame on you, Davie," said his mother. Then she turned to her husband and asked, "Why not, Joe? Why can't they enroll tomorrow?"

"Maybe they ought to, before Davie becomes any more money-mad." And Mr. Harper winked at his younger son.

"Fine, fine. And I hope their parents will be coming to church, not to hear the old minister but to worship God."

When he drove off, the boys' farewell shouts

awakened Helen, who crawled out of bed and called through her open window, "Good-bye, good-bye," without knowing to whom.

"I guess he's right, Joe. We should get into the habit of going to church regularly again," said Mrs. Harper.

"Maybe so." Mr. Harper began rolling up his sleeves. "Only time's precious right now if we're to have any plants."

"Aren't human plants important too?"

He grinned and nodded. "Right, Peggy. Boys, your mother's always right." Then, thinking of Mr. Judson, he said reflectively, "I wish you children had at least one grandfather. You don't know what you're missing."

Timmy wondered what it would be like to have a grandfather and what you missed when you didn't. He decided that if he did have one he'd want him to be just like Mr. Judson. Funny thing about Mr. Judson. He was old—you could tell he was old—but somehow he didn't seem old.

CHAPTER 8.

Timmy, Davie, and Helen, all spick-and-span, were kneeling on the davenport under the front window watching for Mr. Judson. It was shortly before noon on Monday, and he was expected any minute. As it turned out, they had gone neither to Sunday School nor church. Their mother had had a terrible headache that had kept her in bed all Sunday morning; and their father, running around the house with an apron tied under his armpits, had been much too busy to take them.

"Children," he had said at noon, as they ate canned soup, "you have a wonderful mother. I marvel that she can even smile, let alone actually laugh, as I have heard her do on many occasions.

She works from dawn to midnight harder than any galley slave."

But by Monday Mrs. Harper was quite all right; and when Mr. Judson arrived, she made her excuses and promised to do better the following Sunday.

"I hope so," he said in a kindly way. "It's Mrs. Lauderbach's theory that children copy their parents. And maybe other parents will copy you too. There's a lot in example." He smiled down at her, then turned to the impatient children. "The chariot's waiting. Would you young men mind sitting in back and permit me to share my seat with this charming young lady?"

Helen smiled and made her usual speech. "I like you. I like you very much."

"Bless my heart," exclaimed Mr. Judson. "Mrs. Lauderbach claims you're an angel. And I do believe she's right."

While Mr. Judson was helping Helen into the front seat, the boys scrambled into the back. Then, with a final wave to Mrs. Harper, off they went.

The drive to the parsonage was a short one; and a few minutes later, the three Harpers and Mr. Judson were walking up the path leading to the front door. The parsonage was made out of the same dark stone as the adjoining church and from

the outside was rather gloomy-looking. Within, however, it was bright with colorful cretonnes, blooming plants, and Mrs. Judson's warm welcome.

The minister's wife, a plump little woman, reached no higher than his shoulder. She wore her plentiful hair, the color and texture of absorbent cotton, piled high on her head. She had blue eyes and pink cheeks and had, in her own way, as much animation as Helen.

Welcoming Helen, she kissed the little girl's

cheek and pressed her to her bosom, literally smothering the oft repeated phrase, "I like you. I —mumble—mumble—mumble." The boys, on the other hand, Mrs. Judson treated like adults and made no attempt to kiss them, which pleased Timmy very much.

Her welcome completed, Mrs. Judson called her two grandchildren. The boy, Billy, and Davie became friends immediately; but Deborah, who really did look like an angel and who was a little taller than he, quite awed Timmy. Her round eyes were even larger than her grandmother's, her curls of the palest gold. Only in fairy tale books had he ever seen such a pretty girl.

Deborah, too, seemed to be a little shy. She greeted Timmy in a friendly enough way but immediately afterward said, "Pardon me, I must help my grandmother." And she walked away, while Timmy shifted uncomfortably from one foot to the other.

"Maybe you can give me a hand, too," suggested Mrs. Judson, and she put him to work filling the milk glasses and setting out pats of butter.

When they were all seated at the table, Timmy made the mistake of gulping several swallows of tomato juice.

"Don't do that until we have grace," ordered Billy, "and it's my turn."

"He doesn't mean to be rude," apologized his grandfather.

They held hands around the table and Billy shouted proudly, " 'We thank you for the birds that sing, we thank you God for everything.' "

"That's only part of it," complained Deborah.

"I guess God'll get the idea," Mr. Judson said.

During lunch they played twenty questions. When it was Timothy's turn, he took the tiger next door, feeling sure they'd never guess it; but they did quite quickly.

"If a tiger lived in the house next to me, I'd be scared to death," Deborah said, and Timothy decided she was not only pretty but sensible.

After lunch, Davie and Billy settled down on the dining room floor with blocks and Mrs. Judson took Helen into the kitchen to show her how to make a pie in the tin cover of a baking powder can. Deborah and Timothy sat down in the living room and looked into space.

"Why don't you put on your sweaters and go out in the swing?" asked Mr. Judson, taking the afghan from the sofa. "I'm going to take a sun bath."

Glad to have someone suggest *something* they

could do, Timothy and Deborah responded readily to the idea and shortly afterward were pushing themselves lazily back and forth in the double swing. In the garden beyond, Mr. Judson was dozing in a steamer chair.

"Do you like being good all the time?" asked Timothy.

"Me?" Deborah seemed amazed at the question. "I'm hardly ever good."

"What's the worst thing you ever did?"

She thought for a moment. "I guess when I stood on the new chair with muddy shoes. It really was disgusting."

Timothy admired long words and had a collection. "I suppose it was disgusting—unless you didn't realize." Realize was pretty good too.

" 'Course I realized. I did it on purpose, because I was mad. The chair was a delicate pink and my mother told me I was not to sit on it. Well, I didn't disobey. I stood on it."

Timothy laughed boisterously, heedless of the sleeper. "Get a licking?" he asked hopefully.

Deborah nodded. "But that was years ago. I was only a little kid, not much more than eight." Then she went on sadly, "I wish now I'd never done anything in all my life to worry my mother. She's sick. In the hospital."

Timothy remembered when Helen was born and wanted to ask if she was getting a baby, but he decided he'd better not.

"She may go West for a year—a whole year." Deborah's lips quivered. "If the doctor decides she has tuberculosis, she'll have to go."

Timothy stretched out his leg and pushed the swing. For an instant he tried to imagine what it would be like to be away from *his* mother for a year. When he'd been away at camp, it had sometimes *seemed* like a year since he'd seen her. But a whole *real* year—he couldn't let himself think about it. Neither could he tell Deborah how sorry he felt for her. So he just pushed. At length he asked, as if he didn't care at all, "What'll you do?"

"Stay here with Gram and Gramp. Billy'll go to Philadelphia to our other grandparents, and my father will live near my mother in Arizona. He writes, so he can live where he pleases."

"Some mothers go away and leave their children even when they're not sick. I know a girl whose mother went for elephants—"

"I know, Mrs. Gates, who brought back the tiger."

"That's right. Would you really be scared to live next door like me?"

"Indeed I would. I'd never sleep a wink."

She made him feel very brave, for he had slept fine, except for a few bad dreams.

"Are you scared of many things?" he asked.

"Millions."

He liked her better and better. "What, for instance."

"Thunder and lightning and bees and bugs and ants—"

"Ants!" said Timothy. "Not ants!"

"Yes, ants too, the nasty creepy things. I suppose you're not afraid of anything."

He hedged in his answer. "Me? I saw a snake the other day, and I wasn't at all afraid."

"Ugh, don't mention the word. Makes my stomach feel awful. But of course no boy is ever scared."

" 'Course not," he agreed. Then he felt so dishonest that he added, "At least they shouldn't be, but I know a boy who is—who used to be afraid of the stars." His voice had sunk to such a whisper, he had to repeat the last word.

"Stars!" Deborah said scornfully. "What harm can stars do, millions of miles away? A tiny ant, crawling on your hand, is much worse. He ought to be ashamed of himself."

"I'm not so sure of that, Deb," called her grandfather, getting up. He came over to the swing and squeezed into the seat beside her. "I couldn't help overhearing your conversation, and I'd be interested in knowing the boy who's afraid of stars."

"Why, Gramp, you tell me it's wicked to be afraid of anything."

"Not wicked, but nothing to be proud of; and you *boast* you're afraid of ants." He tweaked one of the pale curls playfully. "Now take this boy and the stars. Stars, as you say, are far, far off. They are very orderly, make no noise, merely shine and beautify the sky."

"That's what I say. It's silly to be afraid of them," said Deborah.

Timothy sat with his hands clenched, greatly disliking the discussion.

"On the other hand," went on Mr. Judson, smiling at Timothy, "it shows this boy has imagination, and imagination's a wonderful thing. If the boy could only use his imagination to check his fear . . . I have a little sermon I preach about fear. Deb's heard it, but she enjoys her little terrors."

"Gramp, I do not, but lots of girls are like that."

"Which is where you have it over us. Take your friend, Timmy; I'll bet if he was so scared his teeth chattered, he wouldn't admit it."

"No, he wouldn't," agreed Timothy.

"So you see, he isn't giving in to his fears; he's brave enough to fight them; and if he has enough imagination and intelligence to *be* afraid, he probably has enough to conquer his fears." He broke off abruptly and turned to Deborah. "Deb, my dear, if you would like to teach Timmy chess, you may borrow my carved ivory set."

"Oh, thanks, Gramp. Want to, Tim?"

The boy nodded, anxious to get away from the talk about stars; but Mr. Judson was not ready to let him go.

"Fix up the board, Deb, while I preach my fear sermon to Timmy for his friend, although it never did you any good."

Timothy squeezed over to the corner of his seat, quite sure he did not want to hear a sermon.

"I know a lot about fear myself, because I'm naturally a fearful person," confessed the minister. "As a boy I was always the tallest in my class, and I used to be afraid I'd never stop growing. What makes you stop? I don't know."

Timothy shrugged and grinned. He found it quite pleasant hearing about another boy's fears.

"Ever hear of Gandhi?" asked Mr. Judson.

Timothy wasn't sure.

"He was shot and killed, like Lincoln. Also like Lincoln, he was one of the great, brave men of history. Yet as a child, he used to be so afraid of the dark he had to sleep with the light on. You see, it isn't our fears we need to be ashamed of, but what we do about them."

Timothy nodded, because he thought he was supposed to.

"Let's take the boy who's afraid of the stars," continued the minister. "Maybe he imagines one of them might fall and squash him. Maybe it will, who knows? Tell that boy, Timmy, that as long as we live there are times when every one of us is scared."

"You mean even fathers and mothers?" Timothy frowned.

"Of course. They call it worry, but it's the same thing."

Yes, Timothy had often heard his parents say they were worried about this or that.

"The Bible's full of comfort for fearful people," continued the minister. "Some find the verses for themselves; others like me to pick them out." He took a pad and a flat silver pencil from his pocket. "When I went to college, it was a tossup whether I'd be a minister or a doctor; sometimes I feel like both. Now let me think of a prescription for the boy who's afraid of stars."

"He isn't any more—much," corrected Timothy.

"Good. Fine. But he still has his imagination, and something else will come along to take their place."

Timothy thought of the tiger.

Mr. Judson rocked gently and tapped the paper with his pencil. "I'm like a doctor with a thousand medicines from which to choose, and it's important I select the right one. I prescribed for Deborah, 'Underneath are the everlasting arms.' It was written by Moses. Maybe it gave him courage during the forty years he led his people through the wilderness, and maybe it really is helping Deborah. She's only pretending about the ants; her real worry is her mother."

"Yes," whispered Timothy. "She was very brave about her mother."

"However, that one sounds too girlish for you," Mr. Judson continued. He was silent for a minute, then carefully wrote something on the pad and tore off the sheet. "Here's some stronger medicine for your friend."

Timothy studied the neat printing.

"Let's hear it," suggested the minister.

Timothy read slowly, each word a separate unit.

" 'The — Lord — is — the — strength — of—my—
life,—of—whom—shall—I—be—afraid.' "

"King David wrote that. A brave man, David,
and a brave boy. Remember, he's the one who
killed the giant. Maybe he said to himself when he
put the stone in the sling. 'The Lord is the strength
of my life, of whom shall I be afraid.' "

Timothy thought of Alec and wished he could
be as brave as King David.

"What do you want to be when you grow up,
Timothy?"

"A 'lectrician."

"That's interesting. I often think of God as elec-
tricity, and God's power is inexhaustible. So when
I need more courage, I just say to myself, 'Plug in.'
You know, of course, that a long time ago people
were terrified by lightning. Then came Benjamin
Franklin with his kite—you've heard about him?"

Timothy nodded.

"And Franklin proved that lightning was nothing more than electricity, not something super-
natural, as some people had supposed. Of course,
lots of us are still afraid of lightning, but if we'd
plug in on God—"

"Hey, Timmy," called Deborah. "Aren't you
ever coming?"

"Your master's voice. Guess you'd better go."

"Is it all right?" Timothy hesitated. "Without the sermon?"

"That's my sermon," Mr. Judson said, chuckling.

"Oh." Timothy smiled. "It was nice."

CHAPTER 9.

TIMOTHY'S talk with Mr. Judson had given him a wonderful sense of freedom, like going without an overcoat on the first day of spring. The knowledge that he wasn't so different from other boys and that even grownups were sometimes scared relieved him of a sore burden. He wondered if his father was worried about anything—which meant afraid—and he wished he could tell him about plugging in; but maybe he already knew and that was how he kept so brave.

That evening, before dinner, he took his father to the far end of the garden to show him some crocuses that had struggled through the long grass. No longer did he keep a wary eye on the dividing fence. Let Alec come, and see if he cared. He even went over and shouted belligerently into the woods, "Hi there, Alec!"

"What are you doing, Timothy?" his father asked in surprise. "Spoiling for a fight?"

"I'm not afraid of him."

"Good," said his father, and Timothy caught the pride in his tone. "But why stick your neck out?"

Later, when the children were all in bed and asleep, Mr. Harper asked his wife, "Peggy, where are those boxing gloves?"

"Up in the attic, I think. You're not going to start that again, are you, Joe? Timmy's the wrong kind; he's too gentle, too sensitive."

"Exactly. Therefore he needs lessons."

"Do you *want* him to fight?" she demanded, looking up from her darning with a frown.

"Peggy, he's a natural for every bully. In the city it was Butch; here it's that radio kid. Wherever one goes, there are always bullies. I want him to be able to protect himself."

"And have his eye knocked out in the process?" asked Mrs. Harper.

"Let's hope not. Have you noticed, Peggy, how much older he's grown since we moved here?"

"Older in five weeks! Joe, how silly."

"It goes like that. We run along for a time on an

even plane, then suddenly we're jerked up onto a higher level."

"You consider fighting a higher level?"

"Well, my dear Peggy, it's an achievement to be able to defend oneself."

Mrs. Harper sighed and protested no further.

So the boxing gloves were once more put into use. But try as he would, Timothy could not prevent his father from poking him in the face whenever he chose.

Sunday, making good her promise, Mrs. Harper hustled her three children to Sunday School, saw them settled in their various classes, and then drove back to pick up her husband for church. There was supervised play for the younger children during the church hour, but Timothy was considered old enough to sit through the service. To his surprise, he found he quite enjoyed it. He took a possessive pride in Mr. Judson; that was his *friend* standing up there in the pulpit.

"Isn't that a pretty girl," his mother whispered during a hymn.

"That's Deborah," he whispered back importantly.

Mr. Judson preached on integrity, which means honesty, and Timothy stored the word away, planning to use it on Deborah sometime.

After the service, Mr. Judson greeted them cordially and asked them to stay a minute. He said he had something to ask them. "Also," he added, looking at Mr. and Mrs. Harper, "I'd like you two to meet my wife."

But his wife didn't wait for an introduction. She steamed over, made herself known, and praised the Harper children in such guarded words that they didn't even know she was talking about them.

"It's been decided Deborah will spend a year with us while her mother's out West curing," she said, slipping a plump arm affectionately around the girl's shoulders. "And my husband's planning to give her lessons every day from ten to twelve."

"Not Saturdays," protested Deborah.

"Nor holidays," added her grandmother. Mr. Judson joined them, and she turned to him. "I've told them about your school, Richard, but I haven't extended your invitation."

He picked up the conversation easily, as if he were used to sharing it. "We would like very much to have Timothy join us. How about it?" He looked from one parent to the other.

"Wonderful!" exclaimed Mrs. Harper. "That was to have been my job, keeping him up on his arithmetic and reading, but I've been so busy getting settled."

96

"And you, Timmy? Want to try it?" Mr. Judson turned toward him. "I won't be too strict, and sometimes the teacher won't be there at all."

"I'd like it," Timothy said simply.

"Oh, goody! I'm glad!" exclaimed Deborah, which greatly surprised and pleased him. In fact, he was quite pleased at the whole idea. He hadn't been exactly anxious to start school again, but this was different and might even be fun.

The next morning Timothy walked down to the parsonage for the first lesson. The classes were held in the dining room, with students and teacher grouped around the old and well-scarred walnut table. First Mr. Judson gave each of them five arithmetic examples; Timothy's were easy, and he got all of them right. Next they were left alone to put together a jigsaw puzzle of the United States, each piece being a state. When Mr. Judson returned, he took the puzzle apart and jumbled up the pieces. Then, picking up each piece and holding it wrong side out so they couldn't see the name, he asked them to tell him which state he had in his hand. Each time they recognized the shape of the state and identified it correctly, they were given a credit.

"Now," he said, "you have half an hour to write a letter to anyone you choose, alive or dead: George

Washington, Santa Claus, your mother, whomever you wish. Do the best you can with spelling." He brought the alarm clock from the kitchen and set it to ring in thirty minutes, then returned to his study.

"I'm going to write to my mother," said Deborah and got busy immediately. But Timothy bit his pencil for quite a long while. He would be seeing his mother shortly, so that would be silly. At last he nodded and started in.

"Dear B. Franklin," he wrote. (He was not sure how to spell the first name and decided the initial would do just as well.) "You were very smart. I'd like to make experiments with electricity too. I think electricity is a wonderful thing. I would like to use it to punch a boy. It is better than boxing gloves. When I grow up I am going to study electricity."

The bell rang, so he ended hurriedly. "If you was alive not dead, I would be your friend Timothy Graham Harper."

Mr. Judson rejoined them, picked up the two papers, and read Deborah's aloud first.

"Dear Mommy," she had written, "I am in the dining room writing this letter to you. Gramp has a kind of little school and there is a boy here named Tim. He is my age and nice. He has a little brother five like Billy, and a littler sister, Helen, three, who is very cute. I think little girls are cuter than little boys, but don't tell Billy. Only you can't because he is not with you either. I miss you very, very much, but I do not cry as Billy did when he was here. The clock has rung, so I must close. Love and kisses, Deborah."

"That's a very nice piece of work," commended her grandfather. "Every word is correctly spelled. However, Deb, don't you think the last part might make your mother feel sad? We didn't tell her how much Billy missed her."

"Can't I send it?" said Deborah, looking distressed.

"Maybe I can cut off that part and you can write the finish on the back. Timothy has an excellent letter, too, but I doubt if he plans sending it." He winked at the boy, then read it aloud. Timothy thought it did sound quite interesting.

"There's only one mistake," said Mr. Judson. "You should say 'if you *were*,' not 'if you was.' But there's one thing I don't understand in your letter, Timmy—the part about the boxing gloves."

"Oh, that. My father's teaching me to use them. Which is better, Mr. Judson, boxing gloves or— like you said—plugging in?"

"Better for what, Timmy?"

"For licking Alec, a fresh kid who lives in back of us."

"Not Alec Atkins!" gasped Deborah.

Timothy nodded.

"Why he's awful cute! I listen to him every morning. Do you actually know him?"

"Yeah, and I don't like him."

"In fact, you'd like to pin back his ears," added Mr. Judson.

Timothy giggled at the expression, new to him. "I want to punch him in the nose, that's what."

"I didn't say, Timothy, that plugging in on God was better than boxing gloves for an ambition like that."

"And why should God help you hit a nice boy?" added Deborah.

Timothy looked uncertainly from one to the other. He wished Deborah were not there.

"Just a minute, Deb, leave this to Timothy and me." Her grandfather evidently felt the same as Timmy. He sat down and put the tips of his fingers together in such a way that his hands looked like the steeple of a church. "When I suggested plugging in on God, I meant for courage, not for skill. You need both. But why waste them beating up a neighbor? He'll only come back and beat you up. Wasn't it Abraham Lincoln who said he licked his enemies by making them his friends?"

"I wouldn't want Alec for a friend," Timmy snorted.

"I would. I'd like it very much," said Deborah.

"There seems to be a difference of opinion about this lad, Timmy. Think back. Have you been friendly yourself?"

"Maybe not always," admitted Timothy, recalling the pleasure he had taken in thumping Alec's head on the ground.

"The Bible has something to say about that, too: 'A man that hath friends must show himself friendly.' So before giving this boy a bloody nose, why not try to make him your friend? You might like him on that basis."

Just then the fire horn blasted the noon hour, and Mrs. Judson poked her head through the kitchen door.

"If school's out, a few fresh cookies and a glass of milk never hurt anyone's lunch."

But Timothy heard his mother honking the horn. He jumped up. "I have to go. That's my mother."

"Bring her in. I'm not ashamed of my cookies." Mrs. Judson straightened her apron. "I'll go ask her myself."

Deaf to Mrs. Harper's protests, Mrs. Judson

finally succeeded in getting her to come in and bring Davie and Helen with her; and all seven of them sat around the dining room table eating warm cookies and drinking cold milk. Timmy told his mother what they had studied in class, carefully avoiding the subject of Alec. Fortunately, no one else brought it up either.

When they had finished the platter of cookies and were getting up from the table, Mrs. Harper turned to Deborah and said, "Why don't you come home with Timmy tomorrow, Deborah, and have lunch and spend the afternoon with us?"

"Oh, I'd love to," Deborah said enthusiastically. "May I go, Gram? Is it all right?"

"Why, of course," replied her grandmother, laughing at the girl's enthusiasm.

"Fine. I'll drive down and get both of you after class," Mrs. Harper promised.

While the grownups were exchanging some farewell pleasantries, Deborah drew Timothy aside and whispered to him, "Invite Alec over for the afternoon tomorrow."

"I'll see," he answered vaguely.

"No, promise. Promise, or I won't come."

"Maybe he won't come."

"Do you promise to ask him?"

"All right," Timmy agreed reluctantly.

102

CHAPTER 10.

THAT afternoon Timothy climbed over the back fence and made his way through the woods to the big log house. He was ready to make friends with Alec, even to ask him over, as he had promised Deborah. If that failed, he'd show that big bully he wasn't afraid of him; and if Alec wanted a fight, he'd give him a poke in the nose.

As he neared the house, he wondered if they had a dog—a big police dog or a boxer. He stopped in his tracks, and his heart started up its old tricks. Maybe you were a trespasser when you went to a house uninvited. Maybe he ought to go back and telephone. But beneath the maybes, he knew the truth. He was allowing himself to be afraid. "Plug in," he told himself, "plug in." He continued on his way, feeling empty as a balloon.

Reaching the gate, he again paused momentarily. Then he braced himself and called, "Alec! Hi, Alec!"

"Come in," answered a soft, musical voice.

He went through the gate and for the first time noticed a very pretty young woman lying in a swing on the terrace. She was covered to her chin with a plaid blanket.

"Hello, Pretty Boy," she said, sitting up and pushing the blanket off.

Timmy didn't like being called Pretty Boy, and he backed toward the gate. "If you're sick—"

"Not really. Just sick and tired of dashing all over the map. Sit down. Do you want Alec? He went to his fencing lesson, but he'll be back any minute. Take a chair and tell me your history."

Timmy shook his head. "I haven't studied much history yet."

She laughed. "That's good enough to use on my program."

Could this be Alec's mother, Timmy thought. It sounded like it.

"I'm due at a half-dozen places," she was saying. "But I couldn't possibly cover them all, so I skipped them all. And just as I was getting bored, along you came! Did anyone ever tell you your eyes are frightfully beautiful?"

He shook his head.

"Then neither shall I. Might make you conceited, and there's nothing more odious than a conceited child. Tell me, 'Where did you come from, baby dear?' Don't frown; that's part of a poem. Who are you? A neighbor?"

"Yes, sort of."

"Good. When it gets warm enough to fill the pool, you must come every day and swim with Alec. The only neighboring child I know is that fat girl with the silly mother who shoots elephants and gets her name in the paper by bringing home wild lions."

"A tiger," corrected Timothy.

"Even worse. I warned Alec I'd lick him with a trunk strap if he ever went to that house while it's there. I'm not letting my only child be chewed to death for her publicity."

Her child! So this *was* Alec's mother. Well, he certainly wouldn't want her for *his* mother, Timmy decided. Look at the job she'd done on Alec.

"What do you want to drink?" she was asking him. "Some Choc-o-let?"

"Is that like chocolate?"

"If you listened to me, you'd know it's worlds better. Delicious." She reached over to the glass-

105

topped table and picked up a small brass clown. "Want to press his nose?"

"Why?" asked Timmy guiltily, remembering what he planned to do to Alec if Alec refused to be his friend. "What good would that do?"

"Rings a bell." She pressed it herself and replaced the clown. "It should do some good." Her voice became harsh as she said, "Those lazy, good-for-nothing servants—oh, here she comes."

A maid in a green silk uniform that was as delicate as a spring fern and a white apron that was as frail as Queen Anne's lace hurried over to them.

"One Choc-o-let, May, and for me—oh, make it two. Plenty of whipped cream on his, none on mine."

"Yes, ma'am." The maid headed back for the house.

"Cute, but bone lazy," Mrs. Atkins said in such a loud voice the girl must have heard her. "However, she's better than local help. I had a sitter once, a Mrs. Lauderbach—know her?"

Timmy nodded.

"A circus freak! And she seems to be the best the town has to offer."

Timothy wanted to say he liked her very much, but he kept still.

"I hope you'll come often and play with Alec.

You're such a nice polite boy. He's perfectly terrible. Sometimes I don't know what to do with him."

"Put him to bed without any dessert."

She gave one of her lovely gurgling laughs,

although Timothy hadn't meant to be funny.

"You dear little old-fashioned gentleman! I believe I'll have you on the radio some morning—Alec's friend. Or better still, television. You'd be a knockout on television. Ever hear us in your house?"

"I haven't heard you yet, but I will listen sometime," he promised.

"Will you? Wonderful! You'll swell my audience to a million and one." She paused to direct the maid, who had returned carrying a large silver tray. "Put it here, in front of me, May, and bring over a small table for the young man."

She had the plate of small square cakes, heavily iced and topped with nuts, set on his table.

"Eat all you want," she invited generously. "Does your mother listen to any breakfast couple?"

"I don't think so," answered Timothy.

"We're on from eight until eight forty-five. Be sure you get us. There are the greatest bunch of awful copycats. Makes you sick." She looked at her bracelet watch. "Heavens! Nearly four! I was due at an art opening at three, and I must be there by five." She jumped up, kicked aside the blanket that wound around her bare legs, and clattered off on wooden-soled shoes, calling over her shoulder, "Hang around. Alec will be home any minute."

Timothy studied the cakes and wondered if he should save some for Alec.

A moment later she came clip-clopping back. "I have the most wonderful idea! An Easter party! When is it? About two weeks? Alec'll give it the Saturday before—an egg hunt with Cloverdale eggs—one of Krammer's bunnies for each child. Or perhaps a Dolly Drew Easter egg for the older ones. Won't it be fun?"

"I guess so." Timothy wasn't sure Alec would invite him.

"Loads of fun. I've got to fly. I'll send my secretary down to get your name. Any brothers and sisters?"

"Davie and Helen."

"Fine. We ought to get a big crowd. Tell Keysie about any children you know. I can't trust Alec; he'd bring all the dead-end kids. Bye."

A thin, neat little woman with horn-rimmed glasses joined him a moment later, pad and pencil in hand. Timothy stood up, as he had been taught, and the woman gasped.

"Well, I must say, it's a joy to meet a civilized child." She sat on the edge of a straight iron chair and pushed her glasses higher on her sharp nose. "Mrs. Atkins said to get a party list from you."

"I don't know many; I've only lived here a little

while," Timmy said apologetically. "But there's Charlotte, next door—"

"Charlotte who?"

"Charlotte Gates."

"Oh. Well, I suppose that'll be all right." She made a note in her book. "Go on."

"And Deborah Judson, the minister's grandchild."

The secretary gave a short laugh. "Master Alec's going to be in strange company. Do him good. Go on."

"I have a brother, David Harper. He's five, but he's big for his age."

"We'll include him."

"My sister, Helen; she's only three. I suppose she's too little."

"Is she pretty?"

"Oh, yes, awful pretty."

"We'll put her down. She'll look good in the picture. Go on."

"I'm sorry, but so far that's all I know."

"They'll be the cream of the crop, I'm sure of that. What's your name?"

Timothy told her, thankful Alec wasn't there; and he was only just in time, for a moment later they saw Alec walking across the lawn.

"Here comes m'lord duke," said the secretary with a sniff. Then she called to Alec.

"What do you want Keysie-Wesie?" Alec stopped in his tracks at the sight of Timothy. "Well, little Timid! What d'you want?"

"Alec, don't be rude," scolded the secretary. "He came to visit you, of course."

"What's he drinking?"

"Choc-o-let," Timothy answered for himself.

Alec pressed the clown's nose and tossed a whole cake into his mouth. By the time he could speak again, the maid had appeared. "A cup of that gluck, May, with a big gob of whipped cream. And step on it, you lazy creature."

"Now, Alec," protested the secretary again.

"My mother says she's lazy."

"Your mother says you're to have an Easter party."

"I am? What's that supposed to advertise?"

"It's for fun, Alec, to be neighborly. Do you know any decent children to ask?"

"Plenty. But I'm not asking them. I don't want a party."

"That's for your mother to decide."

"Well, she needn't think she can ask a lot of sissies like Timid. I won't have 'em."

Timothy considered going at once, while the secretary was around; then he remembered he had come to prove he was not afraid. But he was.

"I know what." The secretary closed her book with finality. "We'll ask all the children in your dancing class."

"They're a lousy lot."

"From the one sample I know, it could be," she admitted.

"Just you wait until I tell my mother you said I was lousy," shouted Alec.

The secretary eyed him scornfully, then calmly departed, leaving the boys alone. May's arrival postponed any immediate fight.

"Here you are, Mister Alec. There's a mountain of whipped cream. Hope it chokes you."

"Say, everybody around here's awful fresh. You ought to get fired, May. You all ought to be fired!"

Alec took a big swallow of his drink; and when he set down the cup, he had a large mustache of cream. Timmy laughed boisterously, but the laugh faded when he saw the scowl on Alec's face.

"What's the joke, Timid?"

Timothy shrank into his chair. What had happened to his courage? He couldn't even try to plug in.

Alec finished his drink, got up, and beckoned to Timmy. "Got a little unfinished business with you, Timid."

His mother's voice, soft and lilting, called, "Bye, Alec."

"Thought she'd gone to the city," Alec muttered. Then he called back, "Bye, Mom," and stood still, listening.

Timmy took this opportunity to say hurriedly, "I'm sorry I was nasty about your parents. It isn't nice to be nasty about anybody's parents."

At the slam of a car door, Alec waved Timothy away. "Get along out of here."

"But I just said I was sorry, so why can't we be friends?"

"Go on, beat it," Alec said menacingly.

Friendship had failed. Now was the time to punch Alec's nose. But how could anyone fight when his heart shook his whole body down to his finger tips?

"I'm going, I'm going." Timothy squeezed his shoulder blades together as he made his way past Alec and out the gate. He'd come back someday after he'd had more boxing lessons.

He heard Alec follow him, and just beyond the gate, a punch in the back sent him staggering.

113

Regaining his balance, Timothy gathered his trembling fingers into a fist and swinging around caught his foe on the jaw.

"Why, you fresh kid!" snarled Alec. "I'll show. you."

A punch on Timothy's nose sent the blood spurting.

"Maybe that'll teach you." And Alec returned through the white gate. "Bye, little Timid."

CHAPTER 11.

IN THE morning Mr. Harper usually walked the mile from home to the station. But the trip back was all uphill, so in the evening Mrs. Harper often piled the children into the car and drove down to get him.

On the evening of Tim's bloody nose she left the children in the stationery store to look over the Easter display and went to meet his train alone.

"Joe," she said, as they headed slowly for the store, "Tim's been in a fight again. You ought to see his nose! He won't talk about it, but I did get it out of him that it was that awful Alec."

"So he won't discuss it, eh? Shows he's growing up." And Mr. Harper nodded his satisfaction, which greatly annoyed his wife.

"He won't live to grow up if you don't forbid

that nasty boy to come on our property. Haven't we any rights?"

They paused for traffic. "Are you sure, Peggy, it was all Alec's fault? The other night Timmy seemed to be spoiling for a fight. Maybe he went after Alec."

"Joe, how silly. Can't you do something to keep that bully away?"

Mr. Harper shook his head. "You mustn't try to wrap your boys in cotton wool, Peggy."

"I'm only protecting them while they're little."

"And I'm telling you Tim isn't so little. Leave him alone for a while and see what happens."

"A wonderful idea," she scoffed. "Wait'll he has his neck broken, then do something."

He smiled down at her affectionately. "Bless you, my mother was like you and her mother before her. None of you want to give up your babies. But, my dear, each generation has to stand on its own feet. I'm delighted the boy has so much spunk."

As they approached the car, which was parked in front of the stationery store, they saw that the children had already climbed back in. Mr. Harper waved his paper and called, "Hi, kids!"

"Daddy," said Davie, when his father opened the door, "Alec gave Timmy a bloody nose."

"I told you not to say anything," growled

116

Timothy, crouching in the corner of the back seat and hiding his disfigurement with his hand.

"A bloody nose, a bloody nose," chanted Helen.

"So you went looking for trouble." His father rolled his eyes toward his wife. "What's their house like?"

"Big," said Timothy.

"He saw it before," murmured his mother.

"How come you went over there when you're not the best of friends?" Mr. Harper started the engine.

Timothy shrugged. It would sound pretty dumb to say things went wrong and that he had planned giving Alec the bloody nose. "I just went, that's all."

"You didn't tell me you went over there." Curiosity overcame Mrs. Harper's annoyance. "See any of the family?"

"His mother and the waitress, May, who brought the Choc-o-let, and the secretary."

"Well, you must have had quite a visit. House look nice on the inside?"

"I don't know," he mumbled.

"Timothy," said his mother. "Must you be so close-mouthed?"

"I didn't go in. Just sat on the terrace. His mother's giving him a party. She was going to invite Davie and Helen and me. Now she won't."

"Just as well." Mrs. Harper nodded in satisfaction. "The less you see of that boy, the better. Mrs. Lauderbach says he's terribly spoiled."

"But I want to go to a party," mourned Helen. "I like parties. I want to wear my white dress with blue ribbons."

"Forget about it," Timothy ordered roughly.

After that Timmy refused to say anything further about the incident with Alec; and as soon as he had finished dinner, he went upstairs and shut himself in his room.

The next morning, true to his promise, Timmy tuned in on the Three A's. It was strange and exciting to hear Mrs. Atkins' familiar lilting voice and the same gurgling, musical laugh. He could visualize her as she talked, see her pretty yellow hair, her bright cheeks and white teeth. He wondered what Alec's father looked like. He spoke in a deep rumble and called his wife "dear" and "honey" and "sweet," and she did the same to him. They were very nice to each other. Timmy wondered what made Alec so ugly.

"Just a minute, Alf dear, I want to kiss Alec good-bye." The kiss sounded over the radio. "Bye, little son."

Little—bah!

Oddly enough, even Alec sounded gentle and nice. "Bye, Momsie-Womsie, be good."

"You darling rascal, to say such a thing to your own precious mother. But, Alec dear, you don't have to dash off yet. It's only eight-thirty by Crown, the world's most accurate watch, used by more society women than any other wrist watch. Crown —in six regal designs."

"I like your design the best, Momsie," Alec said as if he had given the matter much thought.

"This is the Empire, but they're all beautiful.

And they are always correct. So linger a minute, son, and we'll talk about the Easter party you want to give."

"Be sure you ask my new friend, Timothy Harper," Alec said.

Timothy drew in his breath. His eyes widened.

"I certainly will, darling. I'll phone him the first thing, and I'll ask his little brother and sister, too."

"I don't care anything about them, but Timothy's a swell guy."

"A nice boy, you mean," corrected his mother.

The nice boy could scarcely believe his own ears.

"Alice," Alf's voice rumbled, "if you don't let Alec go, he'll be late for school."

"Oh, dear, that nasty school." Again she kissed him. "When you get back, darling, I'll make you a hot cup of Choc-o-let. There's nothing more wholesome for growing children." She went on to praise the food value of Choc-o-let and explain how easy it was to make.

"If that isn't the silliest program," protested Mrs. Harper, as she came to the living room door and stood there wiping a dish. "I wish I could make a fortune talking about you children."

But Timothy waved impatiently for silence. How pleasant to know Alec was now his friend.

Alec had threatened to pay him back, and he had. Now it was quits, and they were friends.

The program went on and on, but Alec had left for school and his mother just talked about places she had been and the clothes the people there had worn. None of this interested Timmy at all, so he was glad when they finally signed off.

A few minutes later the telephone rang. When Timothy answered it, a precise voice said, "This is Mrs. Keys, Mrs. Atkins' secretary. May I speak to Mrs. Harper?"

Timothy asked her to hold the wire and dashed into the kitchen. "Mom, quick, it's the secretary, asking us to the party."

"You certainly don't want to go, Tim."

"Yes I do. He's my friend now. He wants me especially."

"I want to go and wear my white dress and blue ribbons," yelled Helen, who had been helping her mother.

So Mrs. Harper went to the telephone and said, yes, all three children would be pleased to accept.

"Oh, dear, Timmy," she said when she had hung up. "You can scarcely squeeze into your best blue suit, and Davie's outgrown his entirely."

"Can I wear my white dress with the blue ribbons? Can I, Mommy? Can I?" Helen cried persistently, pulling on her mother's skirt.

"Yes, dear, but hush a minute." Mrs. Harper reflected a moment, then went on, "Well, I'll have to go to town and buy a new suit for you, Timmy, then Davie can wear your old one. I'll call Mrs. Lauderbach this morning and see what day she can come over. But you'd better hurry now, Tim, or you'll be late for your classes."

When Timothy reached the parsonage, he found that Mrs. Keys had already called there and that Deborah was as excited as Helen over the invitation, though for a different reason.

"It'll make us famous, Tim! I always listen to them if I can, and this morning when they mentioned your name I thought I'd die! Imagine, millions of people heard your name!"

Timothy shrugged as if fame meant nothing to him.

"How do you suppose they knew about me?" asked Deborah.

"I told them."

"Oh, you did." Her voice slid downward in disappointment. "Know who else will be there?"

"Charlotte, next door. A nice kid."

"I know, and I'm glad she's no neighbor of mine. Pretty?"

"She looks like our sitter," said Timothy. "But she's awful nice."

"Who else is coming?"

"Davie and Helen and Alec's dancing class."

"Dancing class! Hum, sounds elegant, doesn't it?"

Timothy shrugged and shifted the conversation to a subject that had been worrying him. He was ashamed that he hadn't kept his promise to Deborah. "I saw Alec yesterday," he said, "but I didn't ask him over. He's awful busy. Fencing lessons and stuff like that."

"Oh, it doesn't matter now," replied Deborah. "I'll meet him at the party anyway." She was so excited that she'd completely forgotten about the promise she'd extracted from Timmy the day before.

It was the following Friday afternoon before Mrs. Lauderbach could come over to stay with the children while Mrs. Harper went shopping for Timmy's suit. She rattled up in her ancient car just after lunch, to be met by a welcoming committee of all three children. They were delighted to see her again and crowded around her excitedly, all talking at once.

Hurrying out to get the car, Mrs. Harper paused long enough to greet Mrs. Lauderbach warmly and to tell her, "I tried to put Helen to bed for her nap to save you the bother, but she insisted on staying up till you came so she could hear one of your songs. She just loves them."

Mrs. Lauderbach beamed her pleasure. She swept Helen up into her arms, kissed each firm, red little cheek, and then said to her, "Well, bless your heart, precious. Aunty Lauderbach will sing you a song just as soon as you say good-bye to your mother."

True to her promise, as soon as the children had waved their mother down the driveway, Mrs. Lauderbach took Helen upstairs, tucked her in bed, and sang her a song. She even stretched a point and did an encore. As usual, Timmy and Davie insisted on listening too.

After they'd all tiptoed out of Helen's room and were downstairs once again, Timothy and David immediately started clamoring for a story. But the sitter had a few things to say first.

"So you kids are goin' to that rowdy's brawl," she said, settling into her chair.

"What's a brawl?" asked Davie.

"It's a rough party, and that's what Alec's will be."

"Not this one," said Timothy. "It's going to be very nice, with an egg hunt and everything."

"Isn't Alec going to be there? You just wait and see." Mrs. Lauderbach snapped a length of thread. "Know about my pet next door?"

"You mean Charlotte?" asked Timothy.

"Yes," said the sitter. "She's gone with her mother on a lecture trip."

"Did they take the tiger?" Timothy seized the idea hopefully, though he'd been too busy recently to think about the tiger very much.

"That they did not. Railroads have some sense. They don't take wild animals that's fed on raw meat."

"So Charlotte will miss the party," Timothy said.

Mrs. Lauderbach shook her head. "She'll be back before Easter, but if I was her mother, I wouldn't let my daughter go to a party given by that savage Alec."

Despite Mrs. Lauderbach's complete disapproval of the Easter party, when Mrs. Harper returned a few hours later, the sitter lingered to admire her purchase.

"Now that's what I call a well-tailored suit. I used to make my boys'." She looked wistful, then broke into a laugh that shook her entire body. "And they looked it. A tailor I never was. I can

125

alter though, and I'm thinkin' them trousers and sleeves will need shortening."

She was right in her prediction, and for the next hour and a half she ripped and stitched and steam-pressed.

"There you are, all ready to wear," she said finally.

When Mrs. Harper paid her, Mrs. Lauderbach shook her head and returned some of the money. "Four hours is what you owe me, not a penny more. Truth is I used to be always doin' for others, same as they did for me, and I miss it. This has been like old times."

"I wish," said Mrs. Harper, as the sitter's car clattered down the drive, "there were more people in the world like Mrs. Lauderbach."

CHAPTER 12.

PLEASE be careful of your new suit, Timmy. It looks so nice on you."

It was two o'clock on the day of the big Easter party, and the three children were undergoing inspection.

"Sure, Mom," said Timmy, strutting around the hall with no small sense of importance, "I'll be careful."

Davie was equally proud of his hand-me-down. "Now I'm as big as you were, Tim," he boasted.

But no one could have been prouder than Helen. She looked down at her dress admiringly and danced around the hall in circles, singing softly to herself, "I have a white dress with blue ribbons, I have a white dress with blue ribbons."

Mrs. Harper smiled, partly because of their

antics but mostly because she was so proud of them all and pleased with the way they looked. "All right, children," she said, "let's go."

On their way to the Atkinses' they stopped to pick up Charlotte, who had returned the day before. She popped out of the door at the first honk of their horn and ran down the steps to the car.

"I hope that fresh Alec acts all right," she said, smoothing the skirt of her blue starched dress as she settled in the back seat between the boys.

"He'll be all right." Timmy spoke with confidence. "We're friends now."

They turned right on the first dirt road and drove a short distance past woods fenced in with split logs until they came to a huge stone gateway. Passing through this, they came out onto a wide paved driveway. Soon the sound of children's voices reached them through the trees, and suddenly the woods gave way to a large clearing. Before them, rolling gently upward to the front of the rambling log house, stretched a wide lawn of bright green, closely cropped grass. The house was even bigger than Timmy had thought; for in the front of the building, a large wing jutted out from each side of the main structure. To the right was a flagstone terrace, with white iron tables and chairs; to the left, a blue-tiled swimming pool.

128

"Oh, charming," exclaimed Mrs. Harper, and Timothy felt as proud as if he had owned the place.

"Mom, that's Mrs. Atkins."

"In the white slacks? She looks like a girl," his mother said with obvious admiration.

"Yeah, she is pretty," admitted Timmy.

May came over to greet them, but Mrs. Atkins, who stood a short distance away talking to several men, didn't even seem to notice they were there.

"Please come for them at five-thirty, ma'am."

Mrs. Harper smiled at May and nodded, then turned to the children and said, "Enjoy yourselves, but see that you act as good as you look." She laughed and slipped in the clutch.

Timothy nodded. It would be easy enough to act right now that Alec was his friend. He waved an impatient good-bye and looked about for his host. Children carrying baskets were scurrying this way and that all over the lawn and in and out of the woods adjoining it. He heard one of them shout, "I've got ten!" The egg hunt must already be on. Where was Alec?

"Stay here," ordered May, walking off.

"Seems they're hunting eggs," said Charlotte. "I wasn't told to bring a basket."

"Me neither," grumbled Davie.

Mrs. Atkins glanced their way and waved to

129

them. But then Helen caught her eye, and she left the men and rushed over to her.

"You beautiful darling! Oh, why wasn't Alec a girl! Come with me and see those nice big men, and they'll take your picture."

She went off with Helen, not stopping to say a word to the others, not even Timothy. He turned his head and scowled at the trees.

A few minutes later, Deborah arrived and walked over to join the two boys and Charlotte. She wore a filmy golden-yellow dress that almost matched the color of her shimmering hair, and she looked even more beautiful than usual.

Timmy was still sulking and was in no frame of mind to remember his manners, so Charlotte had to introduce herself to Deborah.

"Isn't it lovely here," Deborah whispered. "I thought it would be nice, but I couldn't imagine anything so big!" Turning to Timmy, she asked, "What do we do now, Tim?"

Timothy shrugged. "Nothin'," he growled. If only Alec would turn up, he'd see that they took part in the egg hunt.

Mrs. Atkins came over, holding Helen by one hand and extending her other toward Deborah.

"You dear child, what's your name? I want to have your picture taken with Helen and me. Here,

take her coat in for her." She tossed Deborah's coat to Timothy without the slightest glance of recognition and returned to the men with the two girls.

Timothy glared at the coat, uncertain what to do with it, but very sure in his own mind that he did not like Mrs. Atkins at all. He eventually decided to take the coat inside as he'd been told and dodged across the lawn to the open front door. A card table was set up just inside the entrance and blocked his way, so he threw the coat over his shoulder and scrambled under the table into the house. Getting to his feet again, he saw a frowning maid coming down the hall toward him.

"And what do you think you're doin', bustin' into here like that?"

"Mrs. Atkins sent me with this coat." He held it out to her.

"And Mrs. Atkins says you kids is to check your coats here at the door and not come in the house at all. You'll find a little bathhouse by the pool with a room for the boys and a room for the girls." She took the coat. "Now scram."

Timothy scrambled back under the table and made his way across the grass to Charlotte and Davie. He was wishing he had never come to the party. How did he know he wasn't supposed to go in their dumb old house? When people gave parties, they generally let their guests wander all over the house if they wanted to.

May came up to them carrying a circle of baskets in either hand. "Here you are, youngsters," she said cheerfully, distributing them to Timothy, Charlotte, Davie, and a half dozen other newly arrived guests. "Go around to the woods in back and see if you can fill 'em with hard-boiled Easter eggs."

"But are there any left?" asked the doubting Timothy.

"Any left! Bless your heart, we hid a thousand of 'em, all colors of the rainbow—a whole thousand, over twenty apiece. I told 'em in the kitchen we'll be havin' eggplants growing all through the woods." She gave a little laugh.

Timothy, his spirits lighter, ignored his companions and made a dash for the woods, where children were darting every which way. Some had already filled their baskets and had emptied them to collect more.

May hadn't exaggerated. There were plenty! Timothy ran along the path past the others into an untouched area. He found a blue egg, a yellow, a red, another red—he had four, eight, ten! On he rushed getting further and further from the others.

"Hi, Timid!"

That nasty name, and the same ugly voice. Alec didn't sound very friendly.

Timothy turned. He felt a stinging blow on his forehead. A shower of eggshells and a spattering of hard-boiled egg sprinkled all over his new suit. Zing! He caught the second egg with his raised arm. A third smashed against a tree.

Hunching his shoulders, he fled along the path, protecting his head with his hands. Twice Alec hit him on the back, and he knew what that meant—ugly smears on his brand-new suit!

He left the path and ran in and out among the bushes. Ahead he saw the split-rail fence and caught a glimpse of his own barn. Home! A refuge! Safety!

But that would be running away—a cowardly, sissy thing to do. He ducked down behind a bush and tried to quiet his thumping heart. "Plug in for courage," that was it.

He hadn't heard an egg smash for some time, and he suspected Alec had paused to collect more ammunition. Then suddenly he heard the crunching of twigs. Peeking through the thick foliage, Timmy saw Alec approaching warily, peering to the right and left as he came. Timmy tried to forget the pounding in his chest and concentrate on what he should do. He could keep very quiet and

134

hope Alec would pass by without seeing him, then sneak back to the other children; or he could do what his father would prefer—stand up and fight.

Acting on the impulse, Timothy snatched an egg out of his basket, jumped up, and pitched the egg straight at Alec. It caught him square on the chin, and its contents scattered across his mouth and down the front of his suit. Timmy quickly followed it with a second. This smacked against Alec's shoulder.

Crooking his elbow over his face, Alec spun around and ran toward home. Alec running away from him! Timothy felt a rare sense of triumph.

They sped in a zigzag course, Timothy throwing egg after egg, none of which reached Alec. A briar tore Timothy's sleeve, but he had no time to worry about such a trifle.

CHAPTER 13.

THE children, interrupted in their egg hunt, stood on the terrace grouped for a picture. Mrs. Atkins was in the front row, with Helen and Deborah on either side of her.

"Seems too bad not to wait for your son, Alice," the photographer said, walking backward to get them all in the picture.

"No one ever knows where Alec is," she said, frowning. She turned around and scanned the group of children. "Hold your baskets up so they'll show, children. Go ahead, Dick."

The photographer bent his bald head over the camera and squinted through his glasses, blinking nervously. He fussed around for a minute or so more, then seemed to have everything adjusted to his satisfaction. "Now don't move, children," he called to them, "I'm going to snap the—" He was interrupted by the sound of pounding feet, and in almost one motion all the little heads turned to the direction of the sound. The photographer let out an impatient sigh.

"Wait, Dick, here's Alec," Mrs. Atkins called.

"Hold your positions," Dick yelled irritably. "Hurry, Alec."

At that instant a hard-boiled egg seemingly dropped from the sky and crashed smack on the top of the bald head. The egg burst open, scattering bits of red shell and blobs of yellow and white all over Dick's head and shoulders.

"Darnation!" he bellowed, yanking out his handkerchief.

The children yelled and shrieked with mirth. Some of them laughed so hard they had to set down their baskets and hold their stomachs. But Mrs. Atkins looked grim.

"Who threw that egg?" she demanded, her usually musical voice ugly with anger. Unable to make herself heard, she clapped her hands for silence and again demanded, "Who did that?"

Slowly Timothy emerged from the woods, came up to her, and nodded mutely. In his excitement he hadn't realized how close he was to the house.

"Why, you horrid, horrid boy!" She shook his

137

shoulder. "And I thought you were so nice, such a little gentleman. Aren't you ashamed of yourself?"

Timothy saw Alec grinning evilly. "I didn't mean to hit that man," he mumbled.

"You shouldn't have thrown it at all. Those good eggs—it's wicked to waste them. You might have known you would hit somebody."

He could snitch on Alec, say he had started the fight. But that didn't seem very nice.

"Aren't you ashamed of yourself?" repeated Mrs. Atkins.

Timothy shrugged. Helen began to cry.

"I don't wonder you cry, poor little darling, with such a rude brother."

Charlotte, who had edged out of the back row toward Timothy, took out one of her eggs and smashed it on the stone terrace. As if that were a signal, a boy pitched an egg at the gatepost, hitting it a smashing blow; another boy aimed at a tree.

Then eggs started to fly in every direction. Boys and girls alike entered into the wild sport. They aimed at the house, at the white iron furniture, and finally at each other. They ground eggs under their feet, shook them out of their hair, and wiped them out of their eyes.

Timothy, who had no more eggs, ducked behind

the chaise longue on the terrace and peeked above the cushions, stunned by what he had started.

An egg caught Mrs. Atkins on the edge of her shoulder, and she ran into the house crying. The photographer picked up Helen and followed her.

Deborah, who had been hit twice, also sought refuge behind the chaise longue.

"Aren't you awful!" she said to Timmy. "Look at my dress, just look at it." She pointed out a big stain from a glass of grape juice that had been knocked over onto her.

"I didn't do it," Timothy answered.

"Yes you did. You're to blame for all of this. I guess your father and mother won't like it very much when they hear about it."

Timothy looked down at his smeared blue jacket, at the right-angle tear in the sleeve. It would be bad enough when his mother saw him, but if she were ever to learn . . .

"You won't tell them, Deb, will you?"

"No, of course not, but someone will—they always do."

The fight continued unabated, but the scene of battle gradually shifted to the woods as the need for more ammunition arose. Left alone on the terrace, Deborah and Timmy came out of hiding, their shoes crunching the thickly strewed shells.

From the woods beyond, where the rest of the children hunted and hit, hunted and hit, came wild yells and the sound of smashing eggs.

Mrs. Keys came out of the house and viewed the wreck, tight-lipped and speechless.

"Why don't you stop them?" asked Deborah.

The secretary sniffed. "That's what I was sent out to do, but I might as well have tried to stop the Battle of the Bulge. I said it was silly to have so many eggs, but even a thousand can't last forever."

And she was right, for soon the children came streaming back, a band of ragamuffins. Many, like Timothy, had torn their party clothes on briars, and all were besprinkled with bits of shell and lumps of hard-boiled egg. May and Mrs. Keys, each armed with a whisk broom, lined them up and brushed away what they could.

"So you're the little devil who started it all," May said to Timothy, every bit as cross as her mistress. Her whisk broom scratched his neck.

"I didn't mean to," he murmured.

" 'Didn't mean to' don't clean up this mess. I never saw anything like it in all my born days. It's as if the heavens had opened and rained hard-boiled eggs."

Timothy, as clean as May could make him, which was far from perfect, stood aside, his shoulders sagging. The future, as far as he could imagine, held nothing pleasant. He certainly wasn't enjoying this party, but neither did he wish it to be over. The thought of five-thirty and his mother's face when she saw him was horrible to consider, but worst of all was the moment when she would find out what he had done!

Charlotte came over to him and put her plump warm hand in his.

"Know why I threw that egg, Tim?" she whispered. "Because I was mad at her—at the way she treated you. I'm really the one who started the egg fight, and I liked it. It was fun, wasn't it?"

Timothy stretched his mind way back to the moment Alec had turned and run away from him. "Yes," he agreed. "But you didn't really start it." He wanted to say it was Alec, but he held his tongue.

When the last child had been brushed off, Mrs. Keys started a phonograph and told them to follow her around to the front lawn.

Alec, passing Charlotte and Timothy, smirked at them. "Take good care of him, Charlotte. Know his name? It isn't Tim. Oh, no, it's a wonderful name for him—it's Timid."

Timothy hung his head and wondered in misery if Deborah had overheard.

"He isn't either," Charlotte said defiantly.

But Timothy wished she wouldn't stand up for him; he didn't need a girl to protect him.

Alec joined the others, whistling shrilly. But Timothy made Charlotte go on without him. He picked up the whisk broom Mrs. Keys had left and helped May brush off the furniture. The maid ignored him, except for an occasional glare.

A few minutes later Mrs. Keys came out on the terrace. "Oh, there you are," she said to Timmy. "Someone said you'd gone home." She actually smiled. "Come along—refreshments."

"No, thanks."

"No? Why not?"

"*She* wouldn't want me."

"She? You mean Mrs. Atkins? Don't worry about her. She's gone to bed."

"Is she hurt? Really hurt?"

"Not as bad as you I'd say, from the bump on your forehead. It's television night, and she always takes an afternoon nap. So I'm boss and I say, 'Come and get it.' "

Her face had lost its sharpness, and she looked at him almost as if she liked him. Timmy threw down the broom and followed her around to the front lawn, where a long table had been set up. He

142

found an empty folding chair next to his brother and slipped into it.

"You were awful bad," Davie said.

"Don't you say a word about it to mom," ordered Timothy.

While the refreshments were being served, a long blue roadster swung around the drive and stopped a few yards from the table. A tall heavy-set man jumped out. Mrs. Keys hurried over to him and told him something that he evidently thought very funny, for he burst out laughing.

"Hi, children," the man called, walking over to the table. "I hear you've been having quite a time."

Timmy recognized the man's voice . . . it was Alec's father. Mrs. Keys *must* have told him about the fight, but he didn't look upset or angry. He chatted and joked with the children for a few minutes, then called two of the maids over and disappeared into the house with them. When they reappeared, each was carrying a large cardboard box.

"Now, children," Mr. Atkins said, "while you finish your ice cream, we're going to distribute some presents—one for every boy and girl here. Then, when we're finished, we'll all play 'Pin the Tail on the Bunny.' " He started circling the table, dipping into one or the other of the boxes he and the maids were carrying and presenting yellow velvet bunnies to the younger children and big chocolate Easter eggs to the older ones.

Timmy cringed a little as his turn neared. Perhaps Mr. Atkins wouldn't give *him* a present; worse still, maybe he'd give him a bunny instead of a chocolate egg. The mere thought made Timmy's cheeks blaze with shame. But Mr. Atkins greeted Timmy as jovially as he had the other children and to his relief presented him with one of the boxed eggs.

Timothy almost enjoyed the party after that. He thought Mr. Atkins was pretty nice—a lot better than the other two. At five-thirty, though, when the cars started arriving, Timmy's heart hung heavy within him. To make things worse, he noticed that Mrs. Keys was going up to each of the cars and saying something to the parents before they drove off.

When the Harper car pulled up the drive and Timmy saw that his father was at the wheel, he felt a bit easier. But even so, he'd be seeing his mother soon enough.

Timmy scrambled into the car as soon as it had stopped and slumped into a corner of the back seat, waiting expectantly for Mrs. Keys to make her speech to his father. The secretary introduced her-

144

self to Mr. Harper, then laughed and said, "Our egg hunt ended up in a battle royal—with a thousand hard-boiled eggs. But I think the stains will come off."

Not a word about *him*! Timmy shot her a glance of gratitude.

"I must say, kids, you look like a bunch of tramps," Mr. Harper said, turning the car onto the road. "But I can't help wishing I'd been there." He sighed heavily. "A thousand eggs! Whew!"

CHAPTER 14.

NO SAVING sense of humor relieved Mrs. Harper's shocked sensibilities as she viewed the two boys. Their blue serge suits were smeared with egg yolk; egg white was caught in their hair; their socks were down and their shirt collars up. They looked like ragamuffins. But when she saw the right-angle tear in Timothy's sleeve, her mouth set ominously. The boys recognized the expression and knew it meant trouble.

"No use being tragic about it, Peggy," her husband said soothingly. "It's just one of those things —mob violence. They were all in it. Right, Tim?"

"All but Deb," said Timmy, encouraged by his father's championship. "And Helen, of course. They took her away."

"I can't imagine why Mrs. Atkins didn't stop

you," said Mrs. Harper, peeling off Timothy's jacket to study the tear. "Suits don't grow on bushes."

"No, that's where they're ruined." Mr. Harper grinned.

Timothy started to laugh, then thought better of it. The telephone rang, and he hurried to answer it, thankful for the interruption.

"Hello," said a sharp voice. "I want to speak to Mrs. Harper. Is she home?"

He knew who it was and quailed. Why did Mrs. Atkins want to speak to his mother? He yearned to say, "No." Instead he answered, "I'll call her."

"Who is it?" asked his mother, taking off Davie's jacket.

"Mrs. Atkins."

Timothy trailed his mother to the living room and stood by the phone, afraid of what he would hear, but held by grim fascination.

Mrs. Atkins' excited high-pitched voice reached him clearly.

"I thought you ought to know, Mrs. Harper, it was your boy who started that frightful, disgraceful egg fight."

"Little Davie?"

"No, the bigger one."

"Oh, really!" His mother sounded shocked, as

he knew she must be. "I had no idea. I'm very sorry. Very, very sorry."

"You ought to be," said Mrs. Atkins. "And another thing. My Alec tells me he's been very rudely treated at your house. I think it would be better if you kept your boy away from here."

"I shall, Mrs. Atkins, willingly, *very* willingly."

"And it's my advice you punish him severely—ruining a nice party like that—*severely*."

Timothy crushed his elbows against his ribs, but to his amazement, his mother sounded as if Mrs. Atkins had insulted her.

"*That,* Mrs. Atkins, is entirely my affair. Good-bye." Mrs. Harper turned from the telephone and beckoned to Davie. "Come on, you and Tim. I most certainly do not like that Mrs. Atkins."

She took both the boys upstairs and washed their heads roughly, so they knew she was upset. Then she told them to take a shower and went to put Helen to bed—and still not a word about the egg fight.

When the boys came down to the living room in their pajamas and bathrobes, they found their parents reading before the open fire. Timmy's hope that the matter would never be brought up was immediately killed.

"Please, Joe, let me question him," said Mrs. Harper, laying down her paper. "Come here, Timmy."

Slowly he obeyed, eyes on the rug. He hadn't been punished since they'd moved to the country.

"Did you start that egg fight, Timmy?"

He kicked the leg of his mother's chair with his red slipper and said nothing.

"Tell me, Tim. Tell me the truth."

Timothy shrugged. "I didn't mean to hit the photographer."

"It was awful funny." Davie, sitting on a stool, rocked with mirth. "He got it wang on the top of his head."

"Whom did you mean to hit?" continued Mrs. Harper, frowning at David's interruption.

"Alec," answered Timothy.

"Why?"

" 'Cause he'd been chucking eggs at me."

"Who threw the first egg?" His mother eyed him sternly.

"He did. We were in the woods." Timothy felt the bump on his forehead.

"Just what I said," exclaimed his father.

"Exactly, Joe. Exactly. I'm furious!" To Timothy's utter surprise, she suddenly reached out her arms and drew him down on her lap. His thin legs dangled to the floor. "Let me get this straight, Timmy. You say he threw an egg before you did?"

"He sure did." The silk blouse felt soft to his cheek.

"And you didn't tell on him?"

Timothy shook his head. There was something very comforting about his mother's tone.

"Darling, that's wonderful. Perfectly wonderful. We're proud of you, aren't we, Joe?"

At her unexpected praise, Timmy burst into tears. But they were tears of relief. Gradually the misery of the long afternoon gave way to a delightful sense of belonging.

"Maybe you're not as pretty as her." He sniffed and she gave him a handkerchief. "But I'd a million, trillion, zillion times rather have you for my mother."

"You're a discerning young man," his father said. "And as for me, I'm a hungry young man. I haven't been to a party."

That night, thinking how mad Mrs. Atkins would be if she knew he hadn't been punished for the egg fight, Timmy was smiling as he dropped off to sleep.

The next morning, however, a new fear possessed him. Suppose Mrs. Atkins told about the fight over the air and blamed him! It wouldn't be very nice to be disgraced before a million listeners!

Through most of his breakfast, Timmy argued with himself over whether he should listen to the program. It went on at nine on Sundays, and he'd be through eating by then and could sneak up to his room. If she was going to be mean about him, though, he'd rather not hear. But maybe that was cowardly; and after his mother had thought him so

151

brave not to tell on Alec, he wanted to live up to his reputation.

Then he remembered with relief it was his turn to wipe the dishes, so he couldn't listen. After that he devoted all his attention to breakfast and ate his waffles with pleasure.

The hall clock chimed the hour as the two younger children scampered upstairs. To Timothy's consternation, his mother said, "Run along with them, Timmy. I shan't need you."

"There's a heck of a lot of dishes," he argued.

"I know. Your father'll help. I'll call you when it's time to dress for church." And she pushed him gently toward the door as if she wanted to get rid of him.

Timothy mounted the stairs slowly; then, instead of joining Dave and Helen in the attic, he went into his own room, closed the door, and clicked on the radio. There was the voice, sweet as maple syrup. It was hard to realize it could sound as it had over the phone last night.

"Alf, honey, don't you want another cup of coffee?"

Alf most certainly did want another cup of that delicious coffee. "A man who drinks anything else but Silver Brand starts the day with one strike against him," he declared in his deep rumble; and

152

Timothy, sitting tensely on his unmade bed, relaxed for a quick smile. He was nice, that Mr. Atkins.

Alf spent some time praising the coffee, and each passing moment delighted Timothy. Then Alice praised the weather as if it too were one of her products. After that she described what she would wear to church, which took a wonderful amount of time, for she began with her tea-rose nylon slip —told how it was cut, how much it cost, and where it could be bought—and went on the same way through her whole Easter outfit. Alf interrupted her now and then in a clowning effort to describe his undershirt and shorts, and her delicious laugh made him sound quite funny.

Timothy relaxed and lay back on the bed, his ankle propped on his bent knee. Lots and lots of time had passed, and they hadn't mentioned the party. He was sure now they weren't going to. Only fifteen minutes was left of the broadcast. He'd turn it off and go upstairs.

Then he heard Alice say in her cooing voice, "Alec, darling, good morning. He looks all in, doesn't he, Alf? And no wonder, after that terrible party. I scarcely slept all night, and after I'd worked so hard to have it especially nice."

"Forget it, Alice," Alf said.

"I'll never forget it as long as I live. It's terrible to think that one small boy could start all that!"

"Didn't I tell you not to ask him?" said Alec reproachfully.

"But he looks so sweet, dear. I never dreamed he'd be so frightfully rude. I suppose his mother's really to blame, for not training him."

"I only wish I'd been here; it must have been awfully funny," said Alf, laughing.

"It wasn't funny at the time. It was terrifying, like a bad dream. Seems to me a boy who deliberately starts a mob riot like that ought to be sent to a military school to learn some discipline."

"That sissy should be kept in a play pen," said Alec, with a sneer in his voice. "No wonder his name's Timid."

He'd said it! Said that awful word! Timmy had sat up, eyes flashing, when Alec had called him a sissy—*he'd* been the one to run away! But at the sound of that contemptuous word, he shrank back. Suppose someone he knew had heard! And everyone who'd been at the party would know Alec had been talking about him.

Mr. Atkins didn't seem to like Alec's remark either, for he sounded really angry when he said, "Alec! No names now!" But it was too late.

Then Mr. Atkins forgot he was mad and laughed

again. He asked whether there were really a thousand eggs used in the battle, and Mrs. Atkins said there were. She actually giggled when she described the appearance of the terrace after the fight.

"Just the same, I can never forgive the boy who started it," she went on in a subdued tone. Again Timmy held his breath. "Those were Cloverdale eggs. Big, beautiful Cloverdale eggs." She launched into her commercial, and Timmy stopped listening. He sat hunched over, his elbows on his knees, and didn't even notice when the program ended and a crooner came on.

He wasn't a sissy. He shouldn't be kept in a play pen. Worst of all, he wasn't timid, but all his friends who'd heard the broadcast would always think of that when they said his name. Someday he'd show Alec. Maybe he'd kill a poison snake, or maybe the tiger next door would escape and he'd catch it with a net, like the boy in Mrs. Lauderbach's story.

"Children," called his mother, "children, time to dress for church."

She opened his door, heard the radio crooning. "Oh, Tim, you've been listening?"

He nodded.

"Why did you, dear?"

"Wanted to hear."

"Well, they didn't say anything very much. I mean, they didn't mention your name." Timothy stared at the rug. He couldn't talk about it, even to his mother.

"Now it's over and no one was hurt, I agree with Alf. It must have been funny. A thousand hard-boiled eggs, crashing and banging in every direction!" His mother laughed, but it was a mirthless laugh. "Come on, dear, get dressed. First we can make the beds together, you and I."

"I don't want to go to church. It's too hot."

"Hot? It's a perfect day. I mended your suit last night and managed to get them both quite clean."

"But I don't want to go."

"On account of what Alec said?"

He nodded.

"It isn't true, dear." She kissed the scowling forehead. "*He's* the coward. When you get older, you'll find people often blame others for their own weaknesses. Do you remember what his mother said about me?"

Timothy looked up in surprise. "No."

"She said I didn't train you properly—that I was to blame. I could feel worse than you. But I think she's wrong. Just let her wait until you're a great doctor or a judge."

"I'm going to be a 'lectrician," Timothy reminded her.

"All right, that's fine. Come on, dear, give me a hand with the beds."

Timothy obeyed, working mechanically. Nothing his mother could say had the power to take back that shameful word.

CHAPTER 15.

TIMOTHY entered church with his head down, feeling that he would be less visible that way. He kept his eyes focused on people's feet. Must be a big crowd; the feet almost stepped on one another. A lot of flowers, too, especially lilies; for the air was heavy with their scent.

Seated between his father and mother, he studied the hymnal. Once, out of the corner of his eye, he saw Deborah's silver-gold hair; and he felt worse than ever. Her best party dress, spoiled! He wished he might buy her a new one; but by the time he'd saved enough money, he'd be a hundred. He could buy her a box of candy with his savings, though. He had $1.07, which should be enough for a box all fixed up with bows. Not that candy could make up for the dress but it would show he was sorry.

The vibrant organ, which he usually liked, seemed to scold him with its deep rumbles. How many people here knew he was the boy Alec had called Timid?

When the congregation stood up to sing the opening hymn, Timmy was grateful for the human wall that shut him in. Though he kept his eyes glued on the book, he didn't join in the singing. He was wondering whether he might put his dime for the collection plate toward the candy, but he decided that wouldn't be honest.

Usually Timmy took a prideful satisfaction in Mr. Judson's sermons, resenting the slightest cough; but today he spent the time knotting and unknotting his handkerchief. He sat crouched down in his seat, lost in thought, and barely heard a word the minister said.

The minute the service ended, Timmy darted out of the church and ran for the car. He had almost reached it in safety when a boy called, "Hi, you."

Timmy remembered seeing him at the party, the tallest boy there. What chance did he have against a boy that size? But the words sissy, play pen, timid echoed in his ears; and he took a step toward the boy, trying to remember what his father

159

had told him about guarding with his left arm and punching with his right.

"Hello," he answered, watching for the fist to double.

"Some wow, that party, eh?"

The boy actually sounded friendly! Timothy nodded.

"What's your name?"

Now it was coming—jeers like Alec's. Timmy told him, then waited expectantly. But instead of sneering, the boy said, "I'm Frank Harkness, and I'm looking for kids to join our school baseball team. What class are you in?"

When Timothy told him about his classes with Mr. Judson, Frank seemed to be genuinely disappointed. "There's the biggest bunch of kids in this town with tutors. Must be fierce, worse than the darned old dancing class."

"I'll be going to school next September," said Timmy, relaxing.

"Good. Look me up. We need more members, and you ought to be a good runner. Think you'd want to join?"

Timothy's eyes glittered. "Maybe," he said. Suddenly the self-contempt which had shut him in lifted. He saw the beauty of the day, the bright

160

sunshine and dark shadows, the gay Easter hats like bobbing flower gardens. "Maybe I would," he repeated with more enthusiasm.

The next morning Timmy left for the Judsons' earlier than usual to allow time for his purchase at the drug store. He had supposed he could have his pick and selected a flat box ornamented with a yellow bow, only to find it cost $1.50. So he had to be satisfied with a plainer box tied with blue, and even then the druggist let him go in debt eight cents.

Deborah herself answered Timmy's knock at the parsonage door. He didn't say anything about the candy immediately but silently followed her into the dining room, holding the box self-consciously behind his back.

"I'm awful sorry about your dress, Deb," he said finally, in preface to his gift.

"Oh, that. Gram got it all off."

Timothy looked down at the wrapped box, feeling cheated. If her dress was all right, she didn't deserve any candy. He might be able to take it back, or he could keep it for himself or use it to bribe Davie. But he had bought it for Deb, and to keep it from her seemed like cheating.

"Here." He spoke hurriedly so he couldn't

change his mind again. "I got you something in case your dress was spoiled. You can have it anyway."

Her pleasure almost made up for the sacrifice. It was the most beautiful box of candy she'd ever had in her whole life, she said, and dashed first into the kitchen to show it to Gram, then to the study to show Gramp.

Mr. Judson came back to the dining room with Deborah.

"Your parents were more than generous, Tim," he said, nodding toward Deborah.

"They don't know anything about it," mumbled Timothy. "I got it out of my allowance."

"You did?" Mr. Judson took his usual seat at the oval table and studied Timmy carefully for a moment. "Every day of my life I get more sure of one thing," he said. "Timothy, I believe you're going to make a fine man."

"Mrs. Atkins doesn't think so," muttered Timothy.

"Mrs. Atkins!" scoffed Deborah. "I heard her over the radio yesterday, and do you know what I think? I think all of them except Alf—yes, even Alec—I think they're stinkers!"

"Strong language," said her grandfather. "But

I'm glad you can see beneath their glitter. Now let's get to work, children. First the password."

" 'I am come,' " they chanted, " 'that they might have life, and that they might have it more abundantly.' "

"If people would only realize it's the good life that is the abundant life—" The minister thumped the table for emphasis.

"That's right, Gramp," agreed Deborah, who often disagreed with her grandfather. "Tim was good to give me this box of candy, and now I have an abundance of candy. Look, the cover comes off without untying the bow!"

As she replaced the lid, her grandfather winked at Timmy and said, "Maybe when lessons are over, you'll let us do more than *look* at the candy, Deborah." He and Timmy chuckled as Deborah looked at the box with mock sadness.

"Now," said Mr. Judson, "we'll get down to our arithmetic lesson for the day. If you had $1.50 and eggs were—" He paused, looking a little embarrassed, and then they all laughed. "We'll change that from eggs to apples; although apples have been known to do considerable damage too, as for instance?"

"The Garden of Eden?" suggested Deborah.

Mr. Judson agreed with a smile. "Then there's

163

the Greek myth about the three golden apples." He pushed back his chair and crossed his legs, and the children knew they were in for a story.

"Atalanta, a very pretty tomboyish sort of girl, was warned by a fortuneteller never to marry. But lots of young men wanted to marry her; so Atalanta, who could run as fast as a deer, hit on a plan to discourage them. She'd run a race with her suitors; and if anyone could defeat her, she'd marry him. But those who failed must die. Many tried it, but she outran them all. Finally Hippomenes, the judge of the races, decided to try his luck and appealed to Aphrodite—the Greek goddess of love —for help. So—and here come the apples—Aphrodite gave him three golden apples. When they ran the race, each time Atalanta threatened to get too far ahead, Hippomenes threw one of the apples in front of her. She was so fascinated that she stopped to pick them up, and Hippomenes won the race. The odd thing is that Atalanta was glad he'd won."

"Did they marry?" asked Deborah.

"Yes, and they loved each other dearly."

"Why did the fortuneteller tell her not to marry?" asked Timmy.

"The fortuneteller told her that if she ever married, it would bring about her ruin. And the prophecy came true; for shortly afterward, Atalanta and Hippomenes were turned into a lion and a lioness."

Timothy grinned. "If one of them had been turned into a tiger, it might be living next door to me."

"Except that this happened a million years ago," said Deborah.

"Only it didn't really *ever* happen," added Mr. Judson. "But now to get back to our arithmetic lesson—" and he went on with the problem he had started to pose them some minutes before.

This was just the kind of thing that Timmy liked so much about the lessons—they never went in a straight line but sort of zigzagged. Geography got mixed up with spelling and sometimes with arithmetic. Then there was the time they'd been studying about Australia and New Zealand and Mr. Judson had got out *Treasure Island* and read them the first chapter. Timmy thought Mr. Judson was a wonderful teacher.

When he went home that noontime, Timmy took with him a map of Europe pasted to thin plywood, which he had promised Mr. Judson he would cut into countries with his jig saw. He was busy at work on the project after lunch when Charlotte telephoned and invited him and David to come over.

"Can't. Too busy," Timmy said with finality. Not since the arrival of the tiger had he been in her house, and he didn't intend going as long as it was there. "You come over here later—about an hour—and we'll play croquet."

When Charlotte arrived, she was accompanied by her mother. Mrs. Gates, small and trim, with short gray hair parted in the middle and falling into neat waves on either side, didn't look at all like Timmy had thought she would. He found it impossible to imagine her crawling on her stomach in a jungle, carrying a loaded gun.

Mrs. Gates had just returned from Boston that morning and apologized to Mrs. Harper for not having called before. "I'm so glad to meet you and your wonderful family, Mrs. Harper," she said. "Charlotte is devoted to Timothy." Then she caught Davie's big, saddened eyes and added, "And she *loves* Davie."

"And we're very fond of Charlotte," Mrs. Harper replied with something less than her usual friendliness.

"But we don't like your tiger very much," said Davie. "Tim says he's not going in your house, not never."

"I might go sometime," Timmy said, wishing David had kept still.

166

"People make such a to-do over my sweet little Stripy. He's just a darling, darling cat, isn't he, Charlotte?"

"A kind of big cat," replied Charlotte.

Mrs. Gates laughed gently. "I'm afraid my daughter didn't inherit my love of animals. But if you people once saw Stripy, I'm sure you would realize you haven't a thing in the world to fear. He can't possibly get out. He's just as well locked up as if he were in a zoo." She appealed to Mrs. Harper. "You're willing to have the children come over, aren't you?"

Mrs. Harper looked doubtful, as did Timmy. "To tell the unvarnished truth, Mrs. Gates, I'd just as soon they didn't."

For a moment Mrs. Gates looked quite crest-fallen; but then she said brightly, "Would you do me a favor? Come over and look at him. See for yourself how friendly he is and how securely he's locked up. Will you—please?"

Timmy breathed a sigh of relief when his mother said that Helen was napping and that she couldn't leave her.

"We'll wait for her to wake up, and she can come too." Mrs. Gates was not to be swayed.

At that moment, almost as if by signal, Helen called down to her mother from upstairs.

"Good!" exclaimed Mrs. Gates. "Now we can all go; and maybe Charlotte will have a tea party for us."

"She has nice tea parties," said Davie.

"You will come, Mrs. Harper?"

"Why—er—" (Timmy's heart skipped a beat while he waited for her answer.) "Well, all right, Mrs. Gates. Yes, thank you, we'll all go over."

Timmy felt his stomach turn its old somersault. "I saw his room before he came, so I don't have to go. What say to a game of croquet, Char?" He headed for the lawn, but Mrs. Gates called him back.

"Timothy, please. I want you most of all." She smiled at him. "Please come."

"Don't be a sissy," Timothy told himself. "Remember the play pen. Your name is *not* Timid." He drew an uneven breath, looked at Mrs. Gates, and nodded.

So, when Helen was dressed, they all went over to the Gateses', with Helen and Davie leading, the two mothers in the middle, and Timothy trailing behind with Charlotte. What had Mr. Judson told him to say? "The Lord is the strength of my life, of whom shall I be afraid." Yet he *was* afraid.

The group entered the house and started up the stairs, with Timmy still hanging back. His feet

168

made no noise on the thick carpet. I could sneak down again and run home, he thought. But his mother had said he was brave. She was wrong. Alec was right. Alec knew his real name. Timid. But he continued to mount the steps.

Now they were walking down the hall toward the barred door. Timmy followed along, walking more slowly with each step. "Plug in, Timid," he said to himself.

Mrs. Gates carefully let herself through the barred gate. "Nice Stripy," she said soothingly.

Timothy finally edged up to the group around the doorway and forced himself to look in the room.

The large tawny-colored, black-striped animal was much bigger than Timmy had thought it would be. Till now, he had still hoped it might turn out to be just a cub. The restless beast was pacing back and forth against the background of painted trees at the far end of the room, and Timmy followed its graceful movements in fascinated terror. He noticed the play of the muscles in the animal's powerful thighs and shoulders and shuddered. His mouth was dry, and his knees trembled.

Mrs. Gates called to the animal again. "Nice Stripy," she said. "Here, Stripy." The tiger stopped pacing, stood still for a moment, then turned and slunk silently over to its mistress. She put out her hand and stroked its head and back, continuing to speak to it softly. "You beautiful baby! Sweet little Stripy! See how gentle he is?"

"He certainly is a beautiful creature," said Mrs. Harper.

"A perfect specimen," Mrs. Gates said. "He's almost eight feet now and will probably be ten or more when he's full-grown. They want him at the Bronx Zoo when I'm ready to give him up. Stripy, darling, these are your friends. They're not afraid of you."

Naturally Mrs. Gates didn't know he was so scared he couldn't move, Timmy thought. But maybe the tiger wasn't so dangerous after all. How could it be if Mrs. Gates could stand there right next to it and stroke its head like that? This thought made him feel a little better. He hadn't noticed that Mrs. Gates was stroking Stripy with her left hand only and kept her right hand in the pocket of her jacket.

Helen, who'd been quiet up till now, suddenly said, "I love him. I love him. Here, pussy, pussy." She stretched out her hand and tried to get closer to the doorway, but her mother hurriedly pulled back on the hand she was holding.

170

"Timmy's a liar," Davie broke out. "A liar, a liar! He said he wouldn't come here while the tiger was here."

"Hush, Davie," ordered his mother, slipping her free arm about Timothy. "Sometimes it's wise to change our minds."

Timmy wet his lips; he found it hard to make them work. "Mom, you should see Char's playroom! It's swell."

"That's just where we're going now you've seen my playroom," said Mrs. Gates with a smile. "Good-bye, Stripy." She gave the tiger a final pat on the head and slipped out through the barred door, pausing to make sure it was securely fastened behind her. Then they all went upstairs to the playroom and were served refreshments at Charlotte's little table.

On the way downstairs after their tea party, they stopped to look in at Stripy. He was lying in a corner, and in this position did almost look like just an oversized cat. Having survived his first encounter with the tiger, Timmy didn't feel so bad at their second meeting. He thought about how friendly Mrs. Gates had been with the animal and made himself step closer to the door.

"Hello, Stripy," he said gently. "Know me? Nice Stripy." The tiger got up and padded toward him.

Timmy's scalp tingled, but he stood his ground. "Nice Stripy. Maybe I'll bring you a carrot tomorrow."

"Oh, Tim, would you?" Charlotte asked. "Would you really?"

"Yes, I guess so," Timmy replied a little weakly. Why had he said anything like that? Now he'd promised and would have to do it.

The next afternoon, Timmy kept his promise and took Stripy a carrot. His mother, who had been greatly reassured by her visit to the Gateses' the preceding day, offered no objections but told him to be sure not to get too close to the bars.

Charlotte met Timmy at the door, and they proceeded to the tiger's quarters together. As he climbed the stairs, Timmy's heart was beating very fast, but he was determined to keep his word. When they reached the barred entrance, he made sure the tiger wasn't anywhere near the door, then approached it boldly and casually tossed in the carrot.

"It was nice of you to do that, Timmy," Charlotte said. She paused to look up and down the hall, then whispered, "Having you come in and feed Stripy like that makes me less scared."

Timmy was pleased and felt important and brave. Certainly any fears he had felt were well worth the reward of Charlotte's remark. "You shouldn't let yourself get scared, Charlotte. You saw your mother go right in and stroke him."

Charlotte nodded. "She wants me to hold a lump of sugar on my hand and give it to him, but I couldn't do it. Could you, Tim?"

"I guess so—if I had to." He felt, for the second, as if he could do anything. "Hello, Stripy. You know me. Nice Stripy."

The tiger came slinking toward him, and he hoped Charlotte didn't notice how he drew back.

"Now we're friends, Stripy and me, I'll come in and see him often. I guess that'll help you to be brave, Charlotte." He felt like whistling something gay, but at the same time he was a little sorry for Charlotte. "And even if you're not very brave, it doesn't matter so much, because you're a girl. A boy *has* to be brave."

CHAPTER 16.

THE following Friday night after the children were in bed, the Harpers sat in the living room, Mr. Harper reading, she sewing.

"The library's giving a benefit performance of *Snow White* tomorrow." Mrs. Harper matched a pair of plaid socks and rethreaded her needle. "I'm taking Helen and Davie, and I was wondering, Joe, if you and Timmy couldn't do something together."

"My dear, we have plenty to do. Don't worry about that." Mr. Harper turned the page of his paper.

"I don't mean just work in the garden. Joe, you never get anything more than a worm's-eye view of the country."

"Mrs. Harper, you'll have to eat those words."

174

She laughed and looked ruefully at her fingers protruding through the toe of a sock. "Seriously, Joe, it's terribly important for a father to be close to his son."

"I know, dear, and I try; but Timmy likes to keep to himself." Mr. Harper spoke regretfully.

"That's the way I used to be, Joe, awfully shy. The way I suffered! Suppose I pack you a lunch and you two go for a tramp in the Reservation. What say?"

"I say, as usual, the little wife is always right. Let the cutworms cut and the beetles beet." He burst out singing. "Ahunting we will go, ahunting we will go ..."

"Hush, dear, you'll have them all pounding down the stairs."

The next morning at breakfast, Mr. Harper sprang his treat with enthusiasm.

"I've been thinking, Timmy, we've scarcely been off the acre plot. What say if you and I pack some lunch and explore the Reservation?"

"Today?" Timothy asked unhappily. He had planned to put lights on his buckboard, which he had manufactured out of Helen's old baby carriage. The Reservation didn't interest him.

"Yes, today. Your mother's taking Dave and

175

Helen to see *Snow White*, and it'll give us a chance to get away together."

"But I've got some important work to do, Dad."

"So have I, for that matter, but we ought to know something about this part of the country. I found a map of the Reservation—got it right here." He took a map from his pocket and spread it out on the table. "It covers an enormous distance. There's a lake about three and a half miles due north that we might head for—see, here it is—and I guess I'm good for a seven-mile hike. I was brought up in the city, and I don't know much about exploring, but I guess I can learn. We'll take a compass and head due north. Ought to be a lot of fun."

"I'd rather go hiking than see an old movie," growled Davie.

"I'd rather go hikin' than see an old movie," echoed Helen.

Timothy wanted to say, "Take them. I've got too much to do." But he knew Helen could never make seven miles and he wasn't sure about Davie.

"Sorry, youngsters, you're too little," his father said. "When you get as big and strong as Timmy, then you'll have your turn."

Timothy suspected the invitation was much like

one to go on an errand—either you went pleasantly or you were made to go. "What time do we start, Dad?"

"Let's say eleven-thirty. We can walk for an hour or so, then stop for lunch."

"O.K." said Timothy. That wasn't so bad; he would have a lot of time before they left.

A few hours later—shortly before twelve—father and son started out on their adventure. Timothy carried the lunch, and Mr. Harper took charge of the compass and map.

They went around the back of the hedge and crossed over the wide meadow which adjoined the Reservation. Once they were in the woods, the cold air made them glad to have the warm sweaters that Mrs. Harper had insisted they take.

"It's the funniest thing, Tim," Mr. Harper said, as they stopped to put on their sweaters, "how your mother's always right."

He got out the compass and steadied the needle. "A woodsman wouldn't need this. He'd say, 'moss grows on the north side of the trees,' and go by that; but I don't see any moss."

"I do," exclaimed Timothy. "There's some on this tree right here."

"Sure enough," said his father, examining the

tree Timmy had pointed out, "and it's north all right, according to this compass. You use the trees and I'll stick to my instrument."

They located a path that headed in the right direction and followed it until it veered left. Then they struggled through the dense undergrowth for a while till they came upon another trail. This one wound around considerably but seemed to take them more or less in the direction they wanted to go.

Tiny white flowers starred the woods, with here and there a clump of violets or daisies or some other wild flower that they couldn't identify. Once Mr. Harper stopped dead in his tracks and pointed ahead to a delicate green question mark a foot or so high.

"Now what on earth is that?" he asked.

They carefully uncurled a little of the top and decided it must be a fern.

"Cutest thing I ever saw." Mr. Harper shook his head in admiration. "Wonder if your mother's ever seen anything like that."

"I'm going to pick some flowers and things for her on the way back," Timothy said and capered ahead to locate more moss. This was much more fun than he had anticipated.

A short way further on, they found a fallen tree

by the side of the trail and decided it would be a good place to stop for lunch. They were ravenously hungry; and the lunch of ham sandwiches, olives, milk, and apple pie and cheese tasted unusually good to them. After they had eaten, they rested for a while and then started off again. They followed a leisurely pace, with frequent stops to examine some insect or flower or tree that caught one or the other's eye.

When they'd walked for about another hour, Mr. Harper paused to study the compass and map. "We ought to be coming to the lake pretty soon I should think." Timmy climbed up on a rock to look ahead but couldn't see anything except trees.

After another half hour, the guide stopped again and shook his head. "Guess we've walked in scallops, this needle wiggles so."

"We haven't gone very far," said Timmy. "Let's keep going."

And a few minutes later, they were rewarded for their perseverance by the sound of water bubbling and gurgling up ahead. Pushing on, they came to a wide brook that splashed and glittered over a rocky bed.

"If we follow the stream, I bet we'll come to the lake," Mr. Harper said. Then he shook his head at his own suggestion. "No, I guess we can't. The rocks and woods will make the going too hard."

"Let's cross over. The bank looks clearer over there," Timothy suggested.

"Easier said than done," said his father.

"Not for me," Timmy said boastfully. "Look at those stones—we could leap from one to another. It's a cinch!"

"Sure, I could do it easily, with *my* long legs; but the rocks are too far apart for you," his father said. "And if you fell, you'd get pretty soaked."

"But I won't fall. Why should I fall?" A surge of confidence possessed the boy. "Let me, Dad? Let me?"

"Well, we're out adventuring, so go ahead. But be careful. I don't want you to get pneumonia from this trip."

Timmy walked down the bank to the natural stepping stones that crossed the brook. He knew if he were to make it, he'd have to go fast—take it on the leap. He stepped out onto the first rock, then jumped easily from one to another. But out toward the middle of the stream, only the tops of the rocks protruded; and they were further apart than they had looked at a distance. The swirling eddies made him dizzy; water splashed up under his dungarees. But he had to keep going; if he ever stopped, he'd fall for sure.

180

Now he was nearing the farther side, and the going was getting easier again. Then, with a final jump, he landed on the bright green moss of the bank.

"There you are, Dad! Didn't I tell you?" He hoped his father would tell his mother. Lots of kids might have been scared.

"Good work," called his father, starting over.

Halfway across, Mr. Harper paused.

"Don't stop, Dad, take it on the run," yelled Timothy.

But his advice came too late. Mr. Harper's feet slipped off the wet rock, and down he slid into the brook. He flung out his arm to break his fall and in doing so knocked off his glasses, which flew into the shallow water close to shore. Timmy retrieved them while Mr. Harper was floundering to his feet and wading ashore. When he reached the bank, the two of them looked at one another for a moment, then burst out laughing. Their guffaws rang through the still woods.

"And you said *I* couldn't do it, Dad!"

" 'Pride goeth before a fall,' Tim; and that sure was a fall." Mr. Harper slapped the seat of his slacks, making a squishy sound. "Thank goodness the sun is warm. If I could hang my trousers on that branch—"

"Suppose someone came." The idea shocked Timothy.

"Have to take a chance. Here goes." His father

unbuckled his belt. "Without this sopping rag, maybe my shorts will dry."

He wrung the water from his cotton slacks, then stripped off his sweater and squeezed the water from that.

"Did I see you fish out my glasses, Tim?"

"Yes, here they are."

"Good! Fine! Bent but not broken. New lenses would have made it an expensive party." But when he put them on, they reared up from one eye at such a sharp angle that he took them off again and tucked them in his shirt pocket. "It's up to you, Tim, to see any intruder first, if you don't want your poor old father disgraced."

Timothy laughed. Old! Somehow his father had never looked so young—almost like a boy, with his long bare legs, his hair rumpled, and no glasses. And he seemed like a boy, too, entirely different from the businessman who came home on the commuters' train.

"While my wash is drying, Tim, what do you say to a game of mumblety-peg?"

Timothy shrugged. "Never played it."

"Never? Boy alive, what kind of a father have you, anyway? Well, let me get my knife and I'll show you how it goes." Mr. Harper tried to reach in his pocket, and they both laughed as he fumbled about his shorts.

Timmy fetched the knife from the dangling trousers, and they sat down facing each other on the moss. Then his father carefully taught him the various steps of the game, all of which involved tossing or flipping the knife in such a way that it stuck into the ground. Sometimes the knife was flipped with one hand, and sometimes both were used. Timmy thought the names of some of the steps—"spank the baby," "cut the cheese"—were very funny, and he liked the game a lot.

When Timmy had learned all the steps, they played a game. Naturally Mr. Harper won, because he'd had more practice; but he offered to let Timmy escape the usual punishment for the loser.

"Unless you want to learn the whole procedure, son."

Timmy was not sure that he did, but he nodded. So his father picked up a nearby twig, fashioned a peg out of it, and then—with his eyes closed— hammered the peg into the ground with the handle of the knife. Timmy's punishment was to pull the peg out with his teeth.

By the time they'd finished the game of mumblety-peg, it was almost four o'clock and the shadow of the trees was creeping gradually across

184

the brook. Mr. Harper shivered and walked over to get his clothes.

"Guess we'd better be getting home, Tim." He laughed as he pulled on his wrinkled sweater. "Maybe I don't look like a fashion plate, but I hope I can stay as dry as I am."

"Watch me, Dad." And Timmy leaped over the stones to the opposite bank.

"Watch me," echoed his father. "I know the worst that can happen, so I ought to relax—in which case I should be able to do this as well as my son." This time Mr. Harper skipped right across and in a few seconds had joined Timmy on the bank.

The trip home took only half as long; and although they stopped to pick some flowers, they reached the house in a little over an hour. Mrs. Harper and the two younger children had not yet returned.

"Glad we got here first," said Mr. Harper. He looked at himself in the living room mirror and laughed. "It'll give me a chance to spruce up a bit. I don't seem to look my best."

"You look all right to me," Timmy replied.

"Thanks, Tim." He looked at his son fondly. "Can't speak for you, but I've had a very nice day."

"Me too!" Timmy spoke with unusual enthusiasm.

CHAPTER 17.

Early in June, Timothy pulled up his first radish. When he found it not only looked exactly like those his mother used to buy in the city but also tasted the same, he was filled with excitement. He picked a handful and dashed into the kitchen with them.

His mother's enthusiasm equaled his own. "Isn't it marvelous, darling! Such a smart little seed! How did it know enough to be a radish and not a— a beet?"

Timothy knew what Mr. Judson would say— he had heard it often—"God moves in a mysterious way, His wonders to perform." But he shrugged and said to his mother, "It was a radish seed, so it had to be a radish."

He took a bunch to the rectory the next morning; but instead of quoting about God, Mr. Judson told a funny story about a bride who thought radishes grew in bunches all tied with string. That was the way with Mr. Judson. You never could be sure what he'd say.

Timothy enjoyed his lessons at the parsonage. No two days were alike, and it seemed more like play than work. Even arithmetic became a game, one time slanted for Deborah, the next for Tim. That day, for instance, Mr. Judson said, "Here's an engine that can pull a train of ten passenger cars." He paused to draw ten cars on the blackboard. "There are ninety-four passengers in each car. How many passengers on the train?" Then he erased seven of the cars and asked them to figure out how many passengers there were in the remaining ones. All the arithmetic for that day centered on the train. Once while they were busy doing a problem, he added a wild-looking engineer to the train. Timothy shouted with mirth when he looked up and saw it.

The next day Mr. Judson said they would study the cost of making a silk dress for Deborah, and he sketched it on the blackboard. He was obliged to call in his wife to find out how many yards it would take but decided on his own that the material would cost $5.25 a yard. The children found out the cost of the goods, of six spools of silk, of the sash, of the hooks and eyes, and of the buttons. Mr. Judson said he thought a dressmaker would charge $10.00 to make it. Figuring out the entire cost of the dress was their arithmetic problem for the day.

When Mr. Judson saw their answers, which were both the same, he said, "That's wrong."

The children scowled and began adding again.

"No, not you," explained Mr. Judson. "Your answer is right, but it's wrong for a child's dress to cost $41.25. Suppose you write a few paragraphs saying why you think it's wrong."

"But I don't, Gramp, not if you're very rich," protested Deborah.

"All right, then you tell why you think it is permissible. When you've finished, read your papers to Gram. I must go see old Mrs. Farnum. She's leaving for Canada tomorrow."

He often left them in the middle of the morning like that, and Timothy always felt a little lonely when he'd gone.

So the days slipped by; and except for the password, which changed each week, Timothy could not have said what he had learned; but he knew he had a good time.

The lettuce ripened in the garden, and Mr.

Harper was as excited as Timothy over his early peas. But once they had tested the wonders of nature, the boys lost interest and soon found it a chore to keep their little patch weeded.

Badminton became their favorite game and took up most of their time. Charlotte had been given a set for her birthday; and under the tutelage of Hank, the Gateses' chauffeur, they all learned how to play quite well. One week they had a tournament, and there was much excitement over the event. Hank got old Mr. Meggs, the Gateses' gardener, to enter; and Mrs. Gates induced Mrs. Harper to join with her. Timmy persuaded Deborah to play in it too. Mrs. Gates and Hank were the final winners.

One afternoon late in June, Mr. Judson stopped by to see Mrs. Harper. Timmy and Davie were washing up to go over to Charlotte's, and their mother sat under a tree in the yard reading a book.

"I'm in the nature of a walking report card," said Mr. Judson, as they shook hands.

"I hope it's good," Mrs. Harper replied.

"Yes, very good. I might say that I think your son should not only be promoted but should skip a grade."

Mrs. Harper tried not to look as pleased and proud as she really felt. "Oh, really?"

189

Just then the screen door slammed behind Timmy and Davie, and the two boys came scampering across the yard.

"I was just telling your mother, lad," Mr. Judson said to Timmy, "that I'm here to give her a sort of oral report card. And it's good, fine. The point is that I'm taking Deborah over to the school tomorrow to get her entered and graded for September, and I wondered if you'd like to come along.

"I hate to do it," he continued. "It's been a lot of fun for me, my little academy; but I'd be selfish to keep her home next winter. Not that I don't think I could teach her more. Mrs. Harper, I could get them ready for college in no time!" He laughed, and Timmy joined in.

But Timmy laughed to hide his sudden sadness at the thought that he wouldn't be going to the classes at the parsonage much longer. It would be awful going to regular school again, particularly with Alec Atkins there to pick on him the way Butch used to.

"But it's much easier to go to your house," he said to Mr. Judson, still hoping for a possible escape. "It's a couple of blocks nearer, and I've got a good short cut."

"Well, there are lots of advantages in being tutored, Timmy," Mr. Judson replied, "but there are disadvantages too. By going to school, you'll learn one very important thing that I can't teach you—that is, getting along with children your own age. We can't live forever in a little world of our own, you know."

Mr. Judson's voice faded away as Timmy thought how nice it would be if he *could* always live in a world of his own. Maybe he'd marry Charlotte—he'd prefer Deborah but didn't think she'd marry him, so Charlotte would do—and they'd build a little bungalow either behind her chicken house or in her vegetable patch. They'd play badminton every day, and he'd have a big workshop . . .

Timmy snapped out of his daydream when he heard Mr. Judson ask his mother, "Would you like me to take Tim to enroll tomorrow too?"

"Why, yes," his mother answered, "if you're sure it won't be any trouble. Thank you so much for offering. It's very kind of you."

"No trouble at all," Mr. Judson said. "I'll come over after lunch to pick him up." Timmy's heart sank.

"Well, your classes are just about over, Tim. But poor Deb has a slave driver for a grandfather, and she'll be having lessons all summer." He smiled at Timmy and added, "Unless you'd like to come to our summer sessions too. How about it? Want to?"

"Me?" Timmy brightened up considerably. "Yes, I'd like to come."

"Fine. Deborah will be very pleased; and so am I, for that matter." The minister stood up to go, then paused to ask Davie an old riddle. "What's black and white and red all over?"

"Give up," Davie said, after a moment's thought.

When Mr. Judson explained it was a newspaper that was black and white and read all over, Davie looked a little puzzled; but Timmy laughed delightedly, so he did too. Timmy stored the joke away to use on Charlotte.

"That's what's so wonderful about youth," Mr. Judson said to Mrs. Harper. "Everything is brand-new."

The next afternoon, Deborah and Timothy were taken in Mr. Judson's boxy Ford to the Bedford Public School. Timothy found something awesome about the big empty building and the echo of their footsteps on the cement hall.

Mr. Judson had an appointment with the principal, Miss Folensbee, and they went directly to her office. Timmy shivered as they walked in.

"Hello. How's Effie?" Mr. Judson might have been speaking to Charlotte.

192

"All right, Dick, thanks. How are you?" Dick! Even Mrs. Judson called him Richard! "These both your pupils?"

"Yes. Here are some arithmetic papers, and these I suppose you'd call composition. I've given them a spelling test—here it is. Deb is better at spelling than Tim. He's better in math. They know all the states of the Union and all the countries of Europe and their relative positions. They—"

"Just a moment, Dick. Stop bragging. Are you training them to be Quiz Kids?"

He smiled. "Why not? Oh, Effie, if only the Board of Education could afford to have classes of two!"

"And I suppose you'd expect us to get teachers like you," she snapped.

Timothy felt a sudden surge of fury against her. She couldn't speak to Mr. Judson like that!

"Mr. Judson is a very good teacher," he blurted out. No one was as surprised to hear the words as Timmy himself. He hung his head and could feel his face getting flushed. Even so, he wasn't sorry he'd said it. It was true.

Instead of the scolding he expected from her, Miss Folensbee took hold of one of his fists and opening the tense fingers laid his hand on hers.

"That's what I mean, Timothy. We have good teachers here, but I doubt whether in all your life you'll have anyone who comes up to Mr. Judson."

Timmy nodded. He agreed with her absolutely.

"Maybe he's too good," Deborah said petulantly. "I don't want to be shoved up into an upper grade. If you get to college when you're only a kid, you don't have a bit of fun."

Eventually it was decided that Deborah would enter her regular grade and that, with tutoring during the summer, Timmy would be put in the grade above.

Timmy intimated that he'd be very happy to be put in the same class as Deborah—it wouldn't be quite so bad going to a strange school if he had a friend in the class—but Miss Folensbee shook her head. "It wouldn't be good for you or for the others in the class either. Don't you know any of the children in the school?"

"Just Alec Atkins."

"Well, then, you won't feel so strange. If he gets promoted, you'll be in the same class." The principal smiled and Timmy tried to. But he knew without any doubt that he was in for an awful winter.

CHAPTER 18.

SUMMER overtook spring, and the long bright days ripened the boys' carrots and produced buds on Helen's flash marigolds. Timothy found life unusually pleasant, with nothing to worry about until school opened in September. Then one day Charlotte announced that her mother and father had decided to spend August in Scandinavia and that she would be going with them.

Timmy hadn't realized how much of his fun depended on Charlotte—good-natured Charlotte, always ready to play any game, satisfied with any partner. And her mother was so swell too, arranging a tea party for them every afternoon.

"Why do you want to go to old Sweden, Char?" Timothy asked a few days before they were to sail. They were wandering around the lawn, waiting for Deborah to come over to make a fourth for badminton. Davie trailed along behind them, busy with his own world.

"In some ways I'd rather not. I get awful seasick." She patted a tethered lamb that brushed against her leg and added, laughing, "Maybe I could get Mr. Meggs to feed me with the lambs."

"Live with us; we'd have heaps of fun," invited Timothy. Then he remembered he was not supposed to ask anyone to a meal without his mother's permission—just one little meal—and here he was inviting Charlotte for four weeks! So he hastened to discourage her. "But I guess you'd miss your mom and dad and wish you'd gone."

"Maybe I would," she admitted. "What say we get the net up?"

They went in through the French doors of the dining room, leaving Davie playing with a lamb that frisked about on pencil-thin legs.

Deborah joined them in the hall, having come in the front door.

"Hi, kids," she said.

"Hi," they answered. Just then there was a clatter from above, and they looked up to see Hank and Mr. Meggs descending the curved stairs with a large cage.

"Hank," called Mrs. Gates from upstairs, "you'd

better go for the spare tire and come back. Stripy might not enjoy the extra ride."

"Yes, ma'am," answered the chauffeur, feeling for the ncxt step.

"Mother's taking Stripy to the Bronx Zoo," Charlotte explained.

"You mean the tiger's in that box!" Deborah let out a shriek and dashed through the dining room and out onto the lawn. Timmy and Charlotte followed, laughing merrily.

"I'm going to faint! I know I'm going to faint!" Deborah threw herself on the ground.

"Please, Deb, don't be like that," Charlotte begged gently. "There isn't any danger, honestly. He can't get out."

While Deborah was writhing around on the grass, an elegant-looking youth in sport coat and tan slacks appeared from around the garage.

Alec. None of them had seen him since his Easter party.

"Here's Freshy. Send him home, Char," ordered Timmy.

"Can't when I'm hostess," whispered Charlotte.

" 'Course she can't," agreed Deborah, getting to her feet and brushing off the loose grass. She had forgotten how she had felt after the broadcast a few months before.

Alec paid no attention to anyone but Charlotte.

"Hi, Char. Hear you're going to Europe Monday."

"Norway and Sweden," she answered.

"Aw, gee, only there? I'll be in Paris the fifteenth of August. Thought we might meet."

"You certainly have all the luck," exclaimed Deborah, thus making Alec look at her. "I'd rather go to Paris than any other city in the world. Want to stay and play badminton, Alec?"

"Sure, I don't mind."

"We can't play five," muttered Timothy.

"Why not?" asked Deborah. "Davie can be on either side. He doesn't make any difference."

"I play good," said Davie, hurt at her tone.

Alec sneered and said, "Let's get started. Where's the net?"

"No one can get it now." Deborah looked very dramatic. "It's in the closet under the stairs, and the tiger's in the hall."

"Gee!" Alec shied away from the house.

"I'll go for it," Charlotte said.

"No, I will." Timmy started toward the house. "I'm not scared." He'd show that smarty pants. Head high, he stalked over to the French doors.

"Of course there's no danger," he heard Deborah explain. "The tiger's in a crate." Alec gave a scornful laugh.

Tiptoeing across the hall, Timmy heard ominous growls issuing from the cage. He'd never heard Stripy kick up so much fuss before. It took real courage not to run away, and he wished Deborah had kept still.

He tucked the box of rackets under one arm, the net under the other, remembering Mrs. Lauderbach's story about the boy who captured the lion. If that tiger were to escape, he'd show Alec—show the whole world—whether or not he was timid. A shiver of mingled fright and excitement ran through him.

Going over to the cage, he peeked between the closely spaced bars. Two green eyes with great black pupils stared out at him; the lips parted, baring sharp teeth; the tail thumped. Timmy stepped back hurriedly, and his foot kicked something on the floor. He looked down and saw that it was a padlock. Wasn't the door of the cage locked?

He leaned over to get a closer look at the lock and saw that an iron pin held the hasp in place. But if he gave that pin one little yank or just kicked it with his sneaker . . . Of course he'd never do such a thing—it was too wicked—but it would give him

a chance to prove to everyone that he wasn't timid,
that he was really very brave.

"Who's that?" Mrs. Gates called suddenly from
upstairs. "If anyone's in the hall down there, stay
away from Stripy." Timmy was so startled that he
half dropped the net and the box of rackets. He
grabbed them up again and turned to run, not
noticing that the net had caught in the iron pin.
The net started to slip from his grasp, and he
yanked at it frantically. With a jerk it came loose,
and the pin clattered to the floor. The next instant
Stripy sprang out of the cage!

The tiger crouched in the hall for a second, then
leaped toward the front of the house and crashed

through the screen door. Timmy, not quite knowing what he was doing and acting almost involuntarily, dropped the rackets and raced after him, still clutching the net.

Once outside, Stripy bounded down the steps, crouched and looked around, then turned and headed for the rear of the grounds. He shot past the frightened children and past Mr. Meggs and galloped toward the sheepfold.

"Run—the garage!" the gardener yelled to the children, hobbling over to them as fast as he could.

The girls and Davie obeyed; but Alec took to his heels, heading for home, and Timothy continued the chase. He saw the tiger leap into the fold, heard an agonizing cry, and saw it vault the fence again, this time gripping a lamb in its jaws. The little legs kicked helplessly.

"Timmy, come back," called Mr. Meggs. "That tiger's a killer. *Come back!*"

Timothy paid no attention. He knew it was his fault the tiger had escaped. Now he must catch it. He *must!*

Stripy, though he'd been in captivity ever since he was a cub, knew instinctively where to go. He headed straight for the Reservation.

Once the tiger reached the woods, Timothy lost sight of him; but he ran on across the meadow and into the Reservation. He came to the path he and his father had taken the day they'd gone hiking; and he turned onto it, running as hard as he could. But his legs were beginning to pain, and he was gasping for each breath.

Faintly, from far in the distance, he heard someone calling him. "Timothy! Tim! *Timmy!*" Mr. Meggs.

At last, completely breathless and exhausted, he stopped and leaned against a tree, panting. If only he could find some safe place to rest, but there wasn't any. Any second, from any direction, the tiger might spring out on him!

Just then he heard the rustle of leaves behind him. He hugged the net to his chest, trying not to breathe, and slowly turned his head. A chipmunk leaped around a laurel bush and scampered up a tree trunk. Suddenly a bird screeched in the tree above him, and he jumped away. Every wood sound he heard, he thought came from the tiger. A dozen times he heard it—a hundred!

Someone was calling him again. This time it sounded like his mother, but the voice was so faint he couldn't be sure. He imagined himself answering the call. Running back home! His mother holding him close to her crackling starched dress. "It's all right, Tim. You're home, safe!" But he couldn't go back; he had to find the tiger and capture him somehow.

His lungs ceased to pain, and his breath became even. He'd better get started again.

As he gathered up the net and threw it over his shoulder, he tried to remember some of the verses he and Deborah had learned as passwords. Mr. Judson had said that if he or Deb were ever scared, they'd feel better if they just kept saying them over and over again. But his mind was so confused, he couldn't recall a single one. Then the phrase "Plug in" came to him. That's what he had to do—plug in for courage.

He looked about him—woods in every direction. But not friendly woods like they had been when he and his father went adventuring; for somewhere, anywhere, behind a tree, or bush, or rock, crouched a tiger. The dying cry of the lamb rang in his ears. The tiger was a killer!

If he could find the brook again . . . Somewhere he'd heard—probably from Mr. Judson—that animals could find water by instinct. And the tiger might want a drink after . . . after . . . eating. Timmy shuddered. He couldn't bear to think of the poor little lamb. Which one was it? He knew them all by name. He hoped it wasn't Button Nose.

He headed north for the brook, stopping now

and then to look for moss. Gradually the brown
tree trunks, green and golden leaves, and purple

shadows all blended into a single shade of gray.

It must be getting late. He wondered if he could find his way home before dark and wished he had his watch with him so he'd have some idea how much longer it would be light. Maybe he should give up the hunt. It was silly to think he could find a tiger in this big, enormous Reservation! A tiger could run a hundred times faster than he. And it might not have gone north at all. Again he thought of home. Home, safety, the smell of supper, the sizzling of meat cakes . . .

But he couldn't go home until he had trapped the tiger. He was responsible for freeing a killer!

CHAPTER 19.

MRS. GATES had been strangely appre-
hensive all day about taking Stripy to the Zoo; and
she thought the animal sensed her nervousness, for
he was restless and irritable. As the time approached for them to leave, he seemed to get worse;
so she hid a sleeping tablet in the meat that she gave
him just before he was put in the cage.

While Hank was gone for the spare tire, she went
downstairs to see if the pill had calmed Stripy down
at all. But it hadn't. He was growling and thumping his tail against the floor of the cage. She guessed
it was too soon yet for the pill to have taken effect.
Perhaps she should have given him two tablets.
She examined the cage carefully, and it seemed
very secure. But that lock wasn't very good. If
Stripy continued to be so restless, he might work

the pin loose. She'd better go down to the cellar and get a padlock.

She went downstairs and rummaged around in a tool box until she found a good strong lock; but it was closed and she couldn't find the key. Well, probably Hank will know where the key is, she thought, or at least will be able to find one that will fit. So she took the padlock upstairs and put it on the floor by the cage. She checked the pin to see it was in securely, then went upstairs to get her revolver.

As she opened the door to her room, she thought she heard someone down in the hall; and she called out to them to stay away from Stripy. She'd better stay near the cage from now till they left, she decided, to make sure no one bothered him.

There was another noise from downstairs. Immediately afterward the screen door slammed twice in rapid succession. What in the world was going on? Then she heard the children scream and Mr. Meggs yelling something at the top of his lungs.

Suddenly she was panic-stricken. No, it couldn't be that! She dashed to the bureau and snatched the revolver out of the drawer.

The children, the children, she thought, as she ran down the long flight of stairs. Running past the cage, she saw the iron pin lying on the floor nearby. It had really happened! Stripy had escaped!

Outside there was no one to be seen but Mr. Meggs, who was running toward the house. The minute he saw her, he started gesturing wildly toward the rear of the grounds.

"Meggs, the children," she cried, running to meet him.

"Safe in the garage, ma'am—all but that Alec, who must've run home, and Timmy, who's chasin' the tiger."

"Timmy . . . chasing . . . the tiger?" Mrs. Gates repeated incredulously.

"Yes, ma'am. I called him back—I told him the tiger was a killer."

"He's *not* a killer," Mrs. Gates said sharply. "Which way did they go? Into the Reservation?"

The gardener nodded. Then he said, as if he hated to, "Stripy—he killed a lamb—run off with it."

Mrs. Gates, who had started for the woods, stopped dead in her tracks and whirled around. Her face was ashen. "Meggs!" she gasped. "Then he *is* a killer, and Timmy's in terrible danger!"

"Yes, ma'am, I know. If my legs was better, I'd've run after him." The old man cupped his mouth with his hands and yelled helplessly in the direction of the woods, "Timmy, come back. Ti-m-m-y. Ti-m-m-y."

"Never mind. I'll go after him. I know you did the best you could."

At that moment, Mrs. Harper came dashing up the driveway, with Helen in tow. She'd been walking over to see Mrs. Gates and had heard Mr. Meggs calling Timmy.

"Why are you calling Timmy?" she asked, looking at them anxiously. "What's the matter?"

"Stripy has escaped," said Mrs. Gates, trying to hide her excitement and anxiety. "The other children are in the garage, but Meggs says Timmy chased after Stripy into the Reservation."

The blood drained from Mrs. Harper's face, and for a few seconds she stood perfectly still. Then she broke out sobbing and dashed off in the direction of the Reservation. "Tim, Tim, Timmy," she screamed. "Come back! Where are you?"

Mrs. Gates ran after her and caught hold of her arm. "Please, Mrs. Harper, try to control yourself. I'm sure Meggs must be mistaken."

"Let me go—I must try to find him," Mrs. Harper sobbed. "Oh, I can't believe Timmy would do anything so foolish."

"Neither can I," said Mrs. Gates. "That's why I think Meggs must be wrong. Alec was here and ran

209

home, and I think Timmy probably went with him. But I'm going to the Reservation to look for him anyway. Don't get panicky, though, please. I gave Stripy a sleeping tablet earlier, and he'll no doubt just crawl off somewhere and go to sleep."

"Oh, I hope and pray you're right. I'll go call the Atkinses'."

"I'm going after Stripy now," Mrs. Gates said. "You and Meggs get the children into the house and then call the State Troopers immediately. Tell them my tiger escaped while being taken to the Zoo and that he ran into the Reservation. There's a brook about three and a half miles north of here, and I imagine he'll head for that. And you better tell them he's no longer a pet—that he killed one of the lambs." She ran off, calling over her shoulder, "Please try to keep calm. I'm sure Tim's all right."

Mrs. Harper ran back to the house, biting her lips. Stripy had killed a lamb—that meant he must be dangerous. Surely Timmy wouldn't have run after him.

As soon as the hysterical children had been herded into the house and the State Troopers had been notified, Mrs. Harper picked up the phone to call the Atkinses'.

"Timmy's there. He's all right," she said to herself as she dialed the number. Having something to do had helped her to pull herself together. The line was busy. She tried it again and again and a fourth time. Then she was too impatient to wait any longer.

"Meggs, I'm going over to the Atkinses'. Will you take care of the children and make sure none of them leaves the house?"

She ran most of the way, hardly able to stand the suspense. As she approached the house, a second-story screen opened with a bang and Mrs. Atkins poked her head out the window.

"Is it really true? Has the tiger escaped?"

"Yes. Have you seen Timothy?"

"Heavens! Heavens above!" Mrs. Atkins, ignoring the question, began to cry. "When Alec told me, I scolded him—told him I was sick of his story-telling—"

"Have you seen Timmy?" demanded Mrs. Harper. "Please tell me!"

"No, of course not. Oh, what'll I do now?"

"Where's Alec?"

"I don't know. That's the trouble. He went off—mad. You don't really think a cub could do anything dangerous, do you? It was only a pet, wasn't it? Just for publicity?"

"It wasn't a cub any more. And it killed a lamb. I've heard when wild animals taste blood . . . Do you think maybe the boys are together?"

The blond head shook impatiently. "That woman—that awful creature! She ought to be jailed! I'm going to phone my radio station and tell them to broadcast for help." Her head disappeared.

Mrs. Harper sank down on the steps, uncertain what to do and for the moment too weak to move. She heard the sound of a motorcycle and looked up to see a State Trooper coming up the drive. He brought the machine to a stop in front of the steps, dismounted, and walked over to her.

"You live here, lady?"

Mrs. Harper shook her head. "A tiger's escaped—"

"I know all about it, lady. Where do you live?"

"Back, over there." She waved vaguely.

"Well, you better go home. It might not be safe—"

"I can't," she interrupted, wild-eyed. "My boy's off in the Reservation with the tiger."

"So you're the boy's mother—I heard about that. Just the same, you better go on home. We'll find your boy." Then he added dubiously, "If he's really out there."

"Officer, I'm not going home. I can't. I've got to go after him."

"Lady, I've got to see that you get home. Now be reasonable. Want me to waste time arguing with you, when I could be out looking for your boy?"

"No, no, of course not. But I must do something. Can't you understand?"

"Sure I do. But the best thing you can do to help is go home. If you promise to go home and stay there, I can get going. But if you won't go home by yourself, then I'll have to take you."

Mrs. Atkins leaned out the window, and the officer called up to her, "Say, can you drive this lady home?"

"I'll get my secretary to." She ducked inside and called, "Keysie, come take Mrs. Harper home." Then the head popped out again. "Trooper, I'm nearly crazy. I'm Alice Atkins. My boy Alec is off somewhere and a wild tiger—"

"That's what I'm anxious to get looking for. I just wanted to ask if I could cut through your property here."

"Certainly, Officer, go right ahead. Capture it before it hurts my boy, and I'll give you a five hundred dollar reward."

"And please, please get started," begged Mrs. Harper.

213

"Don't worry, lady. I bet you'll find your boy safe at home." He started off toward the rear of the house.

"There's a brook to the north—" Mrs. Harper called after him.

"I know. That's where I'm headed."

Mrs. Keys came out on the terrace as he disappeared around the house. "You poor thing. What a horrible experience for you. But try to believe the best, Mrs. Harper. Try. It does help. I know. My boy was in the war, and he never got a scratch." She led Mrs. Harper to a parked roadster and helped her in.

"I guess I'm not very brave," Mrs. Harper replied. "I used to think Timothy wasn't either. I thought he inherited his timidity from me. . . . It just doesn't seem possible to me that he could have chased that tiger. . . . Maybe he didn't seem very nice at the party, but he's really a wonderful boy."

"Oh, Mrs. Harper, I wish you could have been here! I'll never forget that egg battle as long as I live. I know Timmy's a fine boy, and I certainly never believed he was the one who started the fight."

As they neared the house, mingled feelings of hope and dread filled Mrs. Harper. This was the last straw she had to grasp at.

214

"Do you want me to go in with you, or is there anything I can do?" asked Mrs. Keys.

"No, thank you. Thank you very much."

Mrs. Harper hurried up the path. Over and over she said to herself, "He's home, busy at something, as he always is. Of course he's here. I have only to open the door and call." But in her heart she did not believe it.

Quickly she entered the house and closed the door. Then she called. She called down the cellar stairs, she called upstairs, she ran up to the attic. One last place—the barn. But the barn was empty.

He may have run back to the Gateses'. Of course, that's what he'd do. She telephoned.

Charlotte answered the phone. No, Tim wasn't back; neither was her mother. Dave and Helen wanted to come home. Should she send them with Mr. Judson? "Yes," Mrs. Harper said. "Yes."

She turned on the radio and walked about the room, clasping and unclasping her hands. Music, tuned too high, pulsated through the house. She must have missed the announcement, if they ever gave it.

That Trooper had been cruel, sending her home. Her boy was out in the woods with a tiger! It was enough to drive a mother crazy.

The music ceased suddenly.

"We interrupt this program to make an important announcement. The Bengal tiger brought back from India by Martha Gates, the big-game hunter, escaped today while being removed to the Bronx Zoo. He is a killer. He disappeared into the Reservation in Bedford, New York. Mothers, keep your children in the house. We will keep you informed."

Keep your children in the house.

"Timmy," sobbed Mrs. Harper.

CHAPTER 20.

Timmy, still working his way north, was beginning to think he'd never find the stream. He'd been hunting for hours; and if he didn't find it before it got dark, he'd no longer be able to see the moss on the trees and would have nothing to guide him.

Then suddenly he heard it—the sound of water gurgling over rocks—the sound he'd been listening for, for so long. He broke into a trot and soon saw a break in the trees ahead. Reaching the bank, he looked down and saw a narrow stream flowing lazily through a ravine. This must be part of the same brook that had rushed deep and wide and swift in the spring. Well, it was water, what there was of it; and somewhere along here he ought to find the tiger.

He stuffed the net down the front of his shirt and scrambled down the steep bank, wondering which way to go. Then he remembered something about animals always heading for the hills, so he turned right and headed upstream, walking on the cracked, dry earth of the river bed.

In the trees along the banks birds chirped and called good night messages to each other, quite as if there were not a danger in the world. And Timmy knew what that meant. Soon it would be getting dark. Night! Alone in the woods! Worse, not even alone! If he could only find some place to hide . . . As he trudged along, he carefully scanned the banks and the sides of the river bed, looking for some crack, some crevice that he could crawl in and hide.

Once he stopped briefly to drink some water, hoping it would help the pangs of hunger he was beginning to feel. But the ice-cold water of the brook chilled him; so he got up and hurried on, walking fast to get warmed up.

Then up ahead he saw something that made him scamper over the hard earth and rocks as fast as he could. A small, irregular-shaped cliff jutted out from the bank onto the bed of the stream. It was not the cliff itself that had caught his eye but what he saw in the base of it: a gaping hole that must be

218

the entrance to a cave. A place to hide! It looked pretty small but plenty big enough to crawl in on his hands and knees.

But a few yards from the cave, he pulled up short at the sight of a snake stretched out in the entrance. Just as he noticed it, the snake suddenly flipped sideways and flicked its tail. Then Timmy saw the stripes! That wasn't any snake; it was Stripy's tail!

Timmy's flesh began to creep and he broke out into a cold sweat. "My heart shall not fear," he told himself. "My heart shall not fear." But it did. It thump, thump, thumped against his ribs.

He backed away slowly, scarcely able to breathe, his eyes frozen in terror on the striped tail. Maybe if he spoke to Stripy . . . although Charlotte said wild animals knew people by their smell. Still, he might as well try it. He felt sure the tiger knew he was there anyway, so it couldn't do any harm.

"Hello, Stripy," he said, in a strange, cracked voice. He remembered the times he had stopped before the iron bars to say hello to him. Oh, if those bars only separated them now. He wet his lips and said again, "Hello, Stripy. You know me. Nice Stripy." The tail flicked again and disappeared from view. Was Stripy getting ready to spring out on him?

He stood still, too scared to turn and run, too

scared to move a limb; but nothing happened. Maybe talking to him *had* helped.

But what should he do now? How was he going to catch Stripy? He felt the bulge of the net in his shirt. Oh, it was easy enough in a story, and that had been a fish net anyhow. It was silly to think he could catch the tiger with a badminton net. Stripy could break it in a minute probably. Perhaps he should just sit down where he was until someone found him and let *them* capture Stripy. But maybe the tiger hadn't bothered to come out just because he recognized him. With a stranger he might act quite differently.

But what *could* he do? Mr. Judson said lots of people were afraid—that wasn't important. The important thing was to try to act as you would if you weren't afraid.

He forced himself to take his eyes off the cave and look around at the surrounding area. Nothing but trees, rocks, the banks, the stream. Then he noticed that just upstream from the entrance to the cave was a big rock. It was much too big for him to lift, but if he could somehow roll it down the slope—

Suddenly he had an idea. He edged slowly toward the boulder, saying over and over as he crept along, "Hello, Stripy. Y-you k-know m-me. N-nice

S-stripy." When he reached the rock, he took the big jackknife he used for mumblety-peg out of his pocket and started cutting and digging away the earth around it. He worked as fast as he could without making too much noise. And all the time he worked, he kept repeating the same words, until at last they all ran together, "Hello-Stripy-you-know-me-my-heart-shall-not-fear."

Finally he stood up and getting behind the boulder pushed it with all his might. It didn't budge. So he dug and scratched out more of the earth around it. Then he lay on his back behind it and pushed it with his feet.

"My-heart-shall-not-fear-hello-Stripy-you-know-me." Over and over he said the words, till finally he really forgot to be afraid.

There—it was moving, rocking back and forth a little!

Then, just as he had planned, the boulder turned over down the slope and lodged in the entrance to the cave, hemming in the tiger!

He'd done it! He'd captured the tiger! He, Timothy Harper!

Exhausted by his effort, he lay on the ground for some time. It was too dark to try to find his way home. He'd have to stay in the woods till morning, hours and hours from now. He remembered the night he had been awake with the mumps. Why, a single night could stretch out forever.

A bug crawled over his neck. He brushed it off and got to his feet. Maybe he'd better climb up on the bank—he was getting awfully cold and it might be a bit warmer up there. He picked up the badminton net, which he had tossed aside when he was working, and wrapped it around his shoulders, glad of the little warmth it gave him.

Walking downstream a few yards till he got past the rocky formation of the cliff, he clambered up the bank, grabbing at the exposed roots and scrub to help pull himself up. Then he sat down on a nearby rock to wait.

Gradually the terror and fear began to creep back. Had he really trapped Stripy? Or would he be able to push away the rock? And even if the tiger couldn't get out, the woods must be full of wild animals, dangerous animals. Foxes maybe.

"My heart shall not fear," he repeated. Then he remembered the prayer he said every night. "Dear God," he said, "deliver me from evil." He'd forgotten to plug in—that's why he was scared.

It was now so dark he could barely see his hand in front of his face—he tried it and could hardly see it—but he wasn't afraid. He had plugged in. "My heart shall not fear," and it didn't.

He thought of home, of his comfortable bed, a warm blanket. He made believe he had only to call for his father good and loud and he'd come, preceded by his flashlight, like the night when he'd had that awful nightmare.

Then he saw it! First he thought he must be dreaming; but no, he really did see it! A flashlight!

He scrambled to his feet quickly and shouted, "Here I am! Here I am!"

"Keep calling," a strange voice called. "Am I headed in the right direction?"

"Yes. Come straight. No don't turn. . . . That's right."

In a moment the beam of light flashed directly on him. He squinted into the glare and asked, "Who are you?"

"State Trooper. Your parents are mighty worried about you, son. You should have known better than to go chasing through these woods thinking you could catch that beast. It was—"

"But I did," Timmy broke in.

"You what?" exclaimed the Trooper.

"Caught the tiger. He's down there—trapped in a cave."

"Aw, come on now, sonny—"

"Honest. He's right down there. I'll show you."

Timmy led the disbelieving Trooper down the

bank and pointed out the cave. "I blocked it with a rock."

The Trooper drew his gun and walked up to the cave for a closer look. "Holy Jimminy! How'd you ever do it?"

"Cut the ground away with my knife and pushed it down the slope," Timmy answered. Suddenly he felt weak with relief. It was wonderful to have someone else take charge, especially someone with a light.

"I hand it to you, boy. You're a pretty smart cooky. We'll let Mrs. Gates take care of it from here. I'll signal the others."

"What others?" asked Timmy.

"Everybody. The Fire Department, boy scouts, other Troopers. We've been combing the woods for you for hours." The Trooper put a police whistle to his lips and blew three shrill blasts. "There, that'll do it. One whistle means you're found, two the tiger, and three the whole works." Again he blew three blasts on the whistle.

"Well, kid, I know one thing. Your parents are going to be mighty proud of you!"

Timmy said nothing. Suddenly he realized all the worry, all the trouble he had caused. Suppose he *had* caught the tiger. He was to blame for its getting loose.

224

CHAPTER 21.

TIMOTHY lay motionless, afraid to move, afraid to open his eyes. Foxes, bats, tigers—where was that tiger? Had the rock held? He opened his eyes a crack and saw a ray of sunshine slicing its way between drawn curtains.

Of course. His own room. He had been put to bed there last night, treated like Helen—younger than Helen—like a baby. His mother had undressed him, had called downstairs to hush the confusion of voices, and had tucked him in.

One voice among the many stood out—Mrs Gates. He had heard her say she would never forgive herself. How could she have been so careless?

She didn't know the truth. No one did. He ought to tell, of course, but he couldn't. That was one thing he could never do.

He lay on his back and stared at the ceiling.

"Night, Tim," his father had said. "I'll tell you tomorrow what a swell fellow I think you are."

But his father wouldn't feel that way if he knew the truth. Nor his mother either. She had said, "Darling, I'm so proud of you. You're a wonderful, brave boy." No, he could never, never tell.

Mrs. Lauderbach would think he should—she'd probably blame his mother that he didn't—but she'd be wrong. His mother had told him over and over it was cowardly to let anyone else take the blame for a thing you'd done. Mr. Judson would say he ought to confess too. Probably he'd think it wasn't fair to God. And everyone would agree it wasn't fair to Mrs. Gates.

Nevertheless, he just couldn't come right out and say that it was his fault the tiger escaped.

The door opened a crack.

"Awake, darling?" It was his mother.

He looked around at her and nodded.

"You must be hungry, dear. It's nearly noon."

There were voices downstairs, men's voices. Police? Maybe they knew and had come to take him away to reform school.

"Who's down there?" he asked.

"Reporters. Waiting for you, dear."

"Reporters?" he repeated.

"Yes. They want to hear all about last night. You're famous now, you know. They've been talking about it on the radio and everything."

"Was it on the radio?" he asked dismally. The more people who knew the worse.

"It certainly was. And people have been calling up all morning. You'd better get up now, dear, and come downstairs."

His mother continued to treat him like Helen. She turned on the shower for him, laid out his clothes, and insisted on helping him dress.

"I'll coax your hair to stay parted as long as they're here." She laughed and shook some of his father's bay rum on his hair. "We don't have a hero in the family every day."

He wished she wouldn't talk like that. It made things all the harder.

When he got down to the living room, he found three men and a woman there talking to Helen and Dave.

"Ah," said one of the men, "here comes the conquering hero."

"Yes, this is Timothy." His mother introduced him to the group. "Now, Dave, you and Helen go out and play."

They left lingeringly, with many backward glances. Timmy wished they might stay and he go.

"Sit down, dear," said his mother. "They want
to ask you a few questions."
228

"You may not realize it, young man," another of the men said, "but you did something very remarkable last night."

Timothy stared at him, tight-lipped.

"He's not one to talk about himself," his mother explained.

"Let me handle this, boys," the young woman said. "Now as I understand it, Timmy, you were over playing with the little Gates girl. Mrs. Gates had the tiger brought down to the lower hall, ready to be driven to the Zoo. You went in to get a tennis net—"

"Badminton," Timmy muttered.

"—that's right, a badminton net—when the animal broke out of his cage, dashed through the door, stole a lamb, and disappeared into the woods. And you followed it. Right?"

Timmy nodded. She had skipped over the awful part about how Stripy got out of his cage.

"Look at me, please," called one of the men.

There was a flash of light, and Timmy jumped nervously.

"We'll try that again," said the photographer. "This time I'd like to have you in it too, Mrs. Harper."

"Your mother says they shouted for you to come

back," went on the young woman. "Did you hear them?"

Timmy nodded again.

"What ever made you do such a dangerous thing?"

Timmy stared at the floor sullenly. He wouldn't tell, he wouldn't.

"Do try to be a little more talkative, dear," begged his mother. "These people have come all the way from New York."

"And we have to catch the twelve-forty train back," one of the men added, looking at his watch. "Let me try. How did you think you were going to catch the tiger, Timothy? Had you any idea?"

"Heard a story once. About a boy who captured a lion with a fish net."

"Why, Timmy, I don't remember any story like that," said his mother. "Where did you hear it?"

"Mrs. Lauderbach told it to us."

"So you decided to copy that boy," the reporter went on. "But as the woods grew darker and darker, didn't you feel a little—"

"Let's not go into that, please," interrupted Mrs. Harper.

"Maybe we shouldn't," agreed the man. "For my part, I know I shouldn't have liked it very much, and I don't suppose you did either."

230

"No, I didn't."

"Tell us what happened when you found the tiger."

"I saw his tail. First I thought it was a snake, then I knew better. He was lying in a cave, so I rolled a rock in front of the opening."

"Did it seem long before they found you?"

"Awful long."

"A lifetime to me," added his mother. "It was after ten when I heard over the radio that he'd been found and was safe."

"What happened to Stripy?" Timmy asked, suddenly thinking of a new worry. Mrs. Gates had said he was a beautiful specimen, and if they'd had to shoot him—

"Mrs. Gates finally got him off to the Zoo this morning, thank goodness," his mother answered.

"We've got to skip," one of the reporters said, "if we're going to catch the afternoon editions."

The photographer took a few more pictures and then they left, each one telling Timmy what a fine boy, what a smart lad, what a brave little man he had been.

Even after that, the day continued to be strange and unnatural. The telephone and doorbell rang constantly, and the house was always full of people. About three o'clock, Mr. Judson and Deborah arrived, bringing a lemon meringue pie from Mrs. Judson.

"You're the bravest boy I ever knew in all my whole life!" Deborah exclaimed. "The first *real* hero! Did you see the papers? Gramp says they'll probably have your picture. I'm going to get a scrapbook and keep everything that's printed."

"I'm proud of you, Timmy," Mr. Judson said. "When you were alone in the woods, did you remember to say those verses?"

Timmy nodded, then looked away. It seemed particularly mean cheating Mr. Judson.

"Mrs. Gates just telephoned," his mother said, as Deborah and Mr. Judson drove away. "She's coming over to thank you."

"Won't see her," growled Timmy.

"Darling, she's very upset about what happened. You must try not to hold it against her."

"But I won't see her," insisted Timothy. Not Mrs. Gates—most of all, not Mrs. Gates. "I won't see anybody. I'm tired of seeing people all the time. I want to stay up in my room and read. I want to be left alone."

"Maybe you're right, dear. You need rest and quiet. Come on upstairs. I won't let a soul disturb you."

He made no objection when she suggested he

get into bed. He felt protected from people there. But an hour later, she brought up Dr. Everson.

"I'm not sick," protested Timothy.

"Of course you're not, Timmy," agreed Dr. Everson. "But you've had quite a nervous strain, and we want to find out how the machinery's working."

He felt Timmy's pulse, took his temperature, listened to his heart, and thumped him on the back.

"You're fine as a fiddle. Stay in bed today and tomorrow you'll be ready to hunt lions."

"Oh, Doctor, don't say that." Mrs. Harper shuddered.

Timmy spent the rest of the afternoon alone in his room, but that evening the postponed praises of his father completely destroyed his appetite for supper.

The biggest blow of the day, though, was the news his mother brought when she came in to kiss him good night.

"Mrs. Atkins called a while ago, dear. She asked if you'd be their guest on their program tomorrow, and I said you would."

"No! You didn't! I won't!"

"Timmy, dear, what's the matter with you? You'll only be on for a few minutes, and they'll tell you what to say."

"But, Mother," he begged, "please, I don't want to."

"I thought you'd be feeling better tomorrow, Timmy, and would like to do it. You'll see, you won't mind it a bit." She hugged him tightly. "You mustn't be so shy, darling. If you were brave enough to catch that tiger, certainly a little thing like being on the radio shouldn't bother you."

She didn't know he'd only been brave because he had to, because he had let the tiger loose. He ought to tell her he was a cheat. But he couldn't. He couldn't.

Oh, why didn't they leave him alone!

CHAPTER 22.

ALTHOUGH Mrs. Harper and Timmy arrived at the Atkinses' before seven-thirty, a number of cars were already parked out front and a confusion of voices met them as they entered the house.

"Oh, Timothy, darling!" Mrs. Atkins rushed toward him with outstretched arms. She had apparently forgiven him for the egg fight. "I had the State Trooper who found you on the program yesterday and gave him his five hundred dollars, and I promised my audience I'd try to get you. I can't tell you how many people have phoned to make sure you'd be on. It's simply thrilling!" She smiled at Mrs. Harper. "It's so good of you to share him. You must be a very proud mother."

"I am indeed," Mrs. Harper answered quietly.

"How Mrs. Gates can ever hold up her head again! She might have been a murderer!"

Timmy winced. Probably lots of people were saying things like that about Mrs. Gates, and it wasn't fair. Fortunately Mrs. Atkins didn't say any more about it but rapidly went on to something else.

"I've had a little script prepared for you, Timothy," she continued. "Alec will ask most of the questions. It'll be cute—two pals talking together. I'll go over it with you now."

Mrs. Keys, who was standing at her elbow, handed her a sheaf of papers. Mrs. Atkins riffled through them, pulled out one, and handed it to Timmy. "Now I'm going to take Timothy away from you for a while, Mrs. Harper. Keysie will take you to the library, and you can hear the program in there. And Timothy, you come into the living room with me and we'll just run through this script."

Timmy wanted to run to his mother and beg her to let him go home, but Mrs. Atkins took him by the elbow and led him into the living room.

"Let's sit on the couch over there, Tim," she said to him sweetly. "This is going to be easy as pie. I've had your part typed in red, see?" She pointed to the sheet of paper he was holding. "First

I'll say how proud we all are of you, then I'll ask how you feel, and you say, 'Fine.' Then I'll let Alec talk to you, and he'll say how proud he is to be your friend and ask a few questions. 'About how far did you walk?' And you'll say, 'Seven or eight miles, but it seemed like a million.' You know, keep it light and pleasant. Then Alec will ask how it felt to be alone in the dark woods with a tiger, and you'll say, 'Sort of scary.' Alec'll ask, 'What did you think about?' You'll say, 'I thought of my home, and my bed, and my mother.' True?"

He nodded. He wouldn't bother telling her about plugging in—she wouldn't understand.

"You see how easy it is? Then Alf will say, 'You're rather small fry for all this publicity. Hope it doesn't go to your head.' And I'll defend you. 'Of course it won't, Alf. He's a darling lad.' Then I'll ask, 'How does it feel, Timothy, to be a national hero?' and you'll say, 'I don't know. I just feel like me.' That'll get a good laugh. Oke?"

Timothy shrugged. He hated that part about being a national hero—he didn't feel at all like himself.

"And there you are. It won't take three minutes. At the very end I'll invite you to lunch, and you'll say, 'Thank you. I'd love to come.' Then we'll be off the air, and everybody who hears you will love you and wish you were their little boy. Now we'll go into the studio and run over this with Alec and Alf—have to make it snappy too."

Timmy followed her down the hall to a room in the rear of the house, where Alec and his father were sitting before a table bristling with microphones and several men bustled about testing equipment. A clock with hands as long as Timmy's arm occupied most of one wall.

"Hail to the conquering hero!" said Mr. Atkins.

"Good morning," murmured Timmy.

Alec looked up and growled, "Hi, Tim."

"Hi."

They went over Timmy's part of the script three times. Mrs. Atkins kept interrupting to make him speak louder or with more expression. The third time she said he did very well and hadn't a thing to worry about. How little she knew!

One of the technicians came over to the table and said they would be on the air in two minutes, as they could see for themselves by the big clock. He showed Timmy exactly how close to the microphone he should be and told him not to touch his paper. "Remember, when you're through your part, don't make a sound until I tell you we're off the air."

"Yes, sir," said Timmy.

"I'm opening the mikes," another of the men warned.

He stood at the end of the table, hand raised. When he lowered it, Mrs. Atkins, in her most charming voice, wished her listeners good morning.

"Alf," she said, "let's not keep them in suspense. Yes, I have him here beside me. Timothy's the handsomest little boy you could imagine, with a thatch of dark hair and liquid brown eyes—sometime I must have him on television. It's hard for us to realize that this little lad, who's forever running in and out of the house with Alec (What an awful story—I never was in the house before, thought Timothy), is the same boy who has caught the attention of the entire country by his brave deed. Bedford is proud to have him living here. We are proud to have him as our neighbor. How do you feel today, Timothy?"

The dialogue went along quickly, too quickly. Timmy dreaded the question about how it felt to be a hero. That's where he ought to confess the truth.

When Alec spoke to him, he sounded as if he were actually his friend. But Timmy wasn't surprised; he'd been fooled before.

"It was sort of scary," read Timmy.

Any second now, that awful question. Timmy's knees began to knock together.

The technician nudged him and pointed to his place.

"I thought of my home, and my bed, and my mother," read Timmy.

Now—now! "How does it feel, Timothy, to be a national hero?" Mrs. Atkins asked as if she didn't know the answer. And she didn't really.

Timmy ignored the technician's guiding finger.

"I feel," he said clearly, "like a cheat."

The Atkinses all looked up at him quickly.

"I'm *not* a hero," Timmy went on. "I had to catch the tiger because *I* had let him out of his cage."

Mrs. Atkins gasped. "On purpose?"

"N-no, not really on purpose. But I was standing by the cage thinking that if Stripy escaped and I caught him, then that would prove that I was brave—and—and I guess when I was standing there fooling around, the net—must—have—got—mixed up—with the lock—or something. Mrs. Gates called down and said if anyone was down there to stay away from Stripy and—and—well, I turned to run—b-but something was pulling on the net, so I jerked it. Th-then I heard something drop on the floor—and Stripy jumped out—so it was my fault—not Mrs. Gates's—it wasn't her fault at all."

There, he'd said it! He leaned back against the chair, limp and trembling. His head hurt and he felt sick all over; but he'd said it—he'd told everybody. Now he guessed they'd leave him alone all right.

"Gee, you're some show-off," said Alec, who was forbidden to say anything but his lines. His father gave him a kick under the table.

"Show-off nothing," contradicted Alf. "I'd say, Timothy, you have what's known as guts. I assure you, listeners, this is as much of a surprise to us as it is to you. When you think of it, Alice, that was a remarkable thing for this boy to do. He didn't have to tell anyone. Bet you were amazed, Tim, when that tiger popped out of his cage!"

Timmy nodded, and the technician squeezed his arm. "Yes, awful amazed."

"You felt responsible, so you chased the beast until you found him. Do you know, feller, I'm doubly proud of you. If we all saw our duty and did it like that, this would be a better world."

Mrs. Atkins gave one of her silvery laughs. "Yes, I agree with you, Alf. Timmy's a grand little sport, but please be careful, dear, never again to treat us to such a fright. And speaking of treats, if you've never eaten Kleiner's canned frankfurters . . ." She was off on a commercial.

Timmy, with nothing to say until the end of the program when she invited him to lunch, sat with his chin cupped in his hands, staring at his paper and thinking of his mother in the other room, of his father and Dave and Helen, of Deb—how disappointed they would be. And those reporters! Wouldn't they be furious! Even Mr. Judson and Mrs. Lauderbach would consider him a cheat not to have confessed before. What Mr. and Mrs. Atkins said didn't mean a thing. They *had* to be pleasant over the air.

The program went on and on. Timmy thought it would never end—he wanted to get out of there and go home and be left alone—but finally Mrs. Atkins said, "We're delighted to have had you with us, Timothy. I hope you'll stay for lunch. I think it's your turn, and we're having a lovely salad of Clover Brand peaches stuffed with Blue Medal cream cheese."

Timmy felt a nudge and followed the finger.

"Thank you," he said; but he left out, "I'd love to," for he had no intention of staying.

The Three A's bade their listeners a cheery good-bye, and the man by the clock said, "You're off the air."

"So, you sneaking little cheat," jeered Alec.

"Alec, shut up," roared his father. "The kid's all right."

"Think so?" Mrs. Atkins yelled in a shrill voice. "He cost me five hundred dollars."

"Where's my mother?" demanded Timmy.

"Come along, youngster. I'll take you to her." Mr. Atkins barged out, followed by Timmy.

Mrs. Harper met them in the hall.

"I'm sorry, Mom," said Timmy, seeing her tear-streaked face.

"Darling, darling." She put her arms around him and hugged him. "You have nothing to be sorry about. It was an accident—you didn't do it on purpose. And what you just did was even braver than catching the tiger."

Down the hall, the telephone jangled, and Mrs.

243

Keys hurried over to answer it. "Hello . . . Yes . . . Yes, he's here. I'll call him." She covered the mouthpiece with her hand and called over to Timmy. "You're wanted on the phone, Timothy. Long distance. A woman in Boston wants to tell you how grand she thinks you are."

Timmy went over to the telephone and said faintly, "Hello . . . Yes . . . Thank you. Goodbye."

"I've already had so many calls I've lost track of them," Mrs. Keys said. "And before it rings again, let me tell you what a wonderful young man *I* think you are, Timmy. You—" The telephone interrupted her. "If you don't want to bother, Timmy, I'll tell them you've gone."

"I wish you would, Mrs. Keys," Mrs. Harper said. "I want to get home. I think we'd like to have Timmy alone for a while. And I'm sure his father is anxious to see him."

She and Timmy slipped out the door just in time to escape the radio men, who were coming down the hall to heap their praises on Timmy. But Alf caught up with them as they reached the car.

"Hey, there, what's the rush. I meant what I said on the air, Tim. That was darned brave of you." He slapped Timmy on the back. "I wish you'd come over and go swimming or something with

Alec sometime. Come see me anyway, boy. I'm proud to know you."

As he drove home with his mother, Timmy thought he had never been happier. He had confessed it was his fault; and instead of being treated like a cheat, everyone was even nicer to him. All except Mrs. Atkins and Alec, but that didn't matter. It hadn't been easy to admit the truth, but, oh, how glad he was that he'd done it.

His father and Helen and Dave were waiting for them in the driveway.

"We heard you, Timmy, we heard you," Helen said, jumping up and down. "You sounded just like you. I like you. I like you very much."

"So do I, son. So do I." His father shook his hand and put his arm around his shoulders. "I bet I'm the proudest father in the world right now."

"Gee, Tim, you're swell," was all Davie could say.

"There was a mob of people out here calling for you, Tim," Mr. Harper said, "but I shooed them away—told them we'd like to have you to ourselves for a bit. And the telephone's been ringing constantly. Mrs. Gates called and was so grateful she was almost in tears. She wants very much to see you before she goes. You'll see her now, won't you Tim?"

"Sure—*now* I will," Timmy answered.

Just then they heard the explosive chugging, the rattling and banging noises that could have but one origin. Mrs. Lauderbach's ancient Chevy staggered up the driveway and quivered to a halt.

"Hello, everybody." She struggled out of the car with a baseball bat in her hand. "I just heard Timmy over the air. Now he's what I call a fine feller. I never heard of a boy that would tell on himself like Timmy did. Like I always say, the parents are to blame for good or bad; and you folks must be mighty proud."

She held the bat out to Timmy. "Here's a present—used to be my Jim's. There's a mitt and ball in the car somewhere too. I hear you're going to the public school in September, Timmy boy, and you'll probably be going in for some sports. I imagine the boys'll be wanting you to anyway."

"Thanks a lot, Mrs. Lauderbach," Timmy said, swinging the bat. "Maybe I will." He suddenly remembered the boy who had asked him about being on the baseball team. Yes, maybe he would.

He smiled. Alec could call him what he liked—it didn't matter any more—for deep down inside somewhere, he really did feel brave.